THE DANCER

MAKING MOVES

Seán de Gallaí

Do mo chlann i gCleveland – Ursula, Ben, Muireann,
Fionnuala agus Fraoch.

Seán de Gallai

Acknowledgements

Thanks to my editors Will Mawhood, Robert Doran and Sarah Kettles for proofreading, and Jamie Romain for his creative support and designing the cover. Thanks to Nicole McKeever, Jaqueline Donnellan and Megan Boyda for their advice. Thanks to Darren Maguire, Aislinn Ryan, Ashlene McFadden, Ciara Sexton. Ursula, Alexis, thank you for your encouragement. Lastly, friends and family for their continued support.

Chapter 1

Love it or hate it—but mostly hate it—life was unpredictable. I thought I was awake and alert to everything that happened around me. I thought I was as conscious and mature as one could be at fifteen, but now I knew the true face of reality, and my days of floating trance-like through life were coming to an end. It took a change of environment and a familiar spark to waken me and see the world through different eyes.

That past January, I had been dragged from my home in Kentucky, from Mom, Dad and my beloved little brother, and sent to live with an aunt in Cleveland I had never met before. Nobody explained what was going on or why or for how long, and I woke up in a different house, in a different state, sick and confused, strangers all around me, the heavy winter fog coming at me through the windows. It was a shot of surreal into my veins. Life didn't seem real any more. All I wanted was to be with my family in Alderhill, and I wasn't sure if that would happen.

My time in Cleveland yo-yoed from ugly to beautiful. The ugly won over most times—depressed, missing my parents and my boyfriend Vinnie and constantly worrying about Lucas. But then there were moments of surprising beauty.

I made an amazing new friend, and she was only nine years old. Kate's passion for dance and her skill filled me with a new energy, and when she encouraged me to try, I slowly realized that dancing helped my soul grow, my spirits brighten and my mood soar in ways I could never have imagined. I fell in love with the sometimes furious, sometimes ethereal movements, and I turned to dance when my mind needed peace.

With life out of my control, I concentrated on dance and on helping Kate achieve her dream. Seeing her smile as she lifted her enormous State Championship trophy choked me with tears of joy. Saying goodbye to her after that was tough, knowing I might not see her for a long time, but it was hard for me to be sad about that, knowing I was returning to the family I loved and missed with all my heart.

When Buck pulled up to the gray-white trailer and Lucas came running out, his golden hair falling into his eyes the air caught in my chest. Looking round I absorbed the scene. The grass had grown long all around and Mom's hanging baskets were blooming with color. I thought, Alex, this is the happiest you've ever been.

The first few days home were bliss, hanging with Vinnie by the river, where we would talk and laugh and kiss. In the afternoons, we threw the ball around with Lucas and stayed out to watch the sun go down beyond the alder trees, sucking in the sweet springtime Kentucky air. And being able to sleep in my own bed was the smallest of sweet treats. Those mornings when I dozed, not yet back in school, I lay and thought about the previous months and how I had learned so much about myself having had some time away. But there was one lesson I had learned and deliberately forgotten, and life with all its surprises and unpredictability would not let this lesson go unlearned.

On my fourth night home, the nightmare returned, and my chest was stilled. Lucas dug his nails into my back as he cuddled in my bed for security. We listened to the yelling and the shattering of glass. The room was silent, but the house was alive.

I knew I couldn't lie to myself any more. I stepped quietly out of bed. I needed to see for myself that which I had hidden and locked away.

"Stay there," I said to Lucas. I opened the door, and the yelling and crying came rushing in. A wad of sweat dripped down my face. The door from the hallway into the kitchen was open a crack, and I closed one eye and peered through with the other.

Dad was white and red-faced all at once, and Mom's back was to me. She shouted and shouted at him, and next thing she struck her palm across his face. And it was so loud in the dead of night. Dad clutched his cheek. Mom was quiet a second and my breath was coming quick and shallow. I was afraid they would hear it. Then Mom started yelling again, poking Dad in the chest as he backed away. Lucas began to cry and howl. I found myself cold and frozen where I stood.

I clenched my hands into fists and conjured up the strength to move. I went back to Lucas, into the damp, sweaty bed, and held him tight and whispered into his ears, telling him everything would be alright. It was hard to tell how long had passed before the fighting ended; minutes felt like hours. I hushed Lucas to sleep, but who would comfort me? When I was sure they were asleep, I crept into the kitchen and tapped the Lakewood digits into the phone.

"Hello? It's Alex."

"Is everything alright, honey?"

"John, it's happening again."

I crouched shivering in the kitchen in my night tee, wireless phone pressed against my cheek, saying those words to Uncle Buck. It was extraordinary. For once the world and all its details seemed so vivid — the white tiles with bits of broken green glass, the quiet snores, the smell of crusty pizza and tomato sauce lingering since dinner time. It was like I was a blind person gifted sight. And all the pieces of the puzzle were joining up. This whole time, I had been lying to myself about what was really going on. I had been lying to myself about how bad things were, and Lucas's tears and my salty cheeks proved that.

I always knew my folks liked to drink a little too much and they had their own way of settling arguments, and things weren't always bad. We had food and a warm home. And sometimes things were really great, like when we went camping or to the track or the amusement park. But in Cleveland, Buck and Tammy never argued. My time there had taught me much.

I now understood Grandpa's intentions back in January. He had wanted to get Lucas and me to

Cleveland, somewhere safe for a time, so that they could take care of the termites. Except Mom and Dad were the termites he'd been trying to exterminate. Or at least set straight.

Buck was silent on the phone. Over and over again, I said, "It's happening again." But he was hundreds of miles away. What did I expect?

"I'm so sorry, Alex; I wish I could come straight there and get you. Try and rest, and call Grandpa in the morning."

What could I do? I understood that all families had problems, but there was a right way to do things—not sucking a bottle until your thoughts went black and ignoring the most precious things your stupid mistakes could make. A little boy was owed a good upbringing and an abundance of love. And so was I. Tammy and Buck had helped me see there was a right way, and I was going to show Mom and Dad that they could change and do right by us. With a little bit of help and hard work and understanding, we could be a normal family.

The following morning, golden sun poured through my curtain-less window, and I lay there planning, Lucas snoring quietly.

I poured a bowl of Honey Oats and sat at the kitchen table concentrating on the crunching sounds. Mom stumbled through wearing her pajama shorts and a black tank top, her long legs trying to stabilize. She stared at the floor a minute before her mouth opened so wide I could almost see where her tonsils once lived. She opened a fresh bag of coffee with a sharp knife. Trapped air hissed its way to freedom. Then she pressed go on the machine, and soon the gurgling and dripping started and that smell filled the room. I clinked my spoon into the bowl when I had finished. Mom turned.

"Oh, Alex honey. My, I didn't even notice you," she said in a sickly-sweet voice. I noticed dried blood on the back of her right hand, and the strands of hair falling down around her face were all stuck together. I gritted my teeth. She came and kissed me on the cheek, but my body was cold.

"Honey, your hair is all messed up short like that. I hope it don't take long to grow back. Your face looks like one of them aliens; you know it looks much prettier when it falls around your face. You're getting tall and real pretty, just like I used to be."

My breathing was shallow.

Mom poured oil on the frying pan. I could hear her groaning over the sound of crackling eggs. I left my bowl by the sink as she hunched over the counter top holding her head.

"Sweetheart. Will you get your momma some medicine from the bathroom cabinet? Poor Momma got one of her migraines."

"Sure thing," I said, all cheery.

"And tell your pa his breakfast is cookin'."

She could get her own medicine. I went in search of Dad.

Mom's room was surprisingly clean all for the stale alcohol sweat stench. The bed was empty.

The porch door slammed shut behind me with a squeak. Harper scampered over, figured where I was headed and led the way, wagging his stumpy tail. The beat-up maroon Camry had only made it a hundred yards up the dirt track. Harper jumped up at the driver door, clawing and scratching just like Dad hated. His figure lay hunched over the steering wheel. A big wad of drool hung from his open mouth, ready to drop. I tapped on the window.

"Dad, wake up. DAD!"

One eye opened and angled across in my direction. He peeled his face off the rubber steering wheel and rolled down the window.

"It's morning already?"

"Dad. We need to talk," I said, all strict. He rubbed his face and held his head in both hands like Mom had earlier.

"Well sure, honey, we can talk. What you want to talk about?" He tapped the passenger seat with his hand and smiled. I raised my eyebrows.

"Dad. You know what I'm talking about." I nodded to his lip.

"Oh, that's nothing. You know how frisky your Mom can be. She don't mean nothing by it, really."

"Really? I heard you say she was out of her mind. We need to do something."

"Oh nonsense, it'll be fine. We got this far, didn't we? I mean, you turned out ok, didn't you?" he said, smiling. He could find a funeral amusing if he wanted. I frowned the biggest my face would allow. "This what marriage is all about. My dad and mom were just the same, and pretty sure so was your grandpa, down the road."

"Dad, we need to find some solutions. You were in the army. Did they train you to lie down like a dog and not stand up for what's right?"

He exhaled long and hard and rubbed his face some more. "My god! My head feels like an explosion."

An explosion? I asked myself. I was lucky I could tie my own shoelaces. My gene-pool seemed starved of intelligence.

"Ok, Alex. Get me a beer, and let's talk this through."

He mirrored my glum expression. I let him dwell on his words a minute, and when I spoke next, it was soft.

"Dad, it's not ok for Mom to hit you." He didn't reply. "And you know, all this drinking and arguing. It's not good. Lucas is frightened for his life. And so am I. Is that ok with you?"

"Come on, Alex, it's not like we always drinking and hollering. Just sometimes…"

"Sometimes is too many times," I said, my arms stretched, palms offered to the heavens. My voice went all lyrical like Mom's did, and I hated myself for doing that.

"Your mom's just having a hard time is all, since she got fired from Applebee's. She'll get another job soon, and things will be better. Your momma don't do so well idle."

"And how about you, Dad? It's Monday. Shouldn't you be at work?"

"It's a long weekend, honey," he grinned. I gave him a look, and he became serious. "What? I ain't kidding. The boss told us to take Monday. We worked hard to finish a job, and we start a new project tomorrow. Things gonna go back to normal. Don't worry."

But I felt on edge. Was Dad's idea of 'normal' good enough for me anymore?

That night we all sat down to microwave lasagna and garlic bread. Mom popped the cap off a bottle of beer, and Dad cast his eyes up at her while stuffing his face. My heart fluttered.

"Sorry, Joe, it's the last one. You didn't buy none, did you?" She waited for him to respond; he didn't. "Thought so. Well, I ain't sharing."

Nobody said much during dinner, and I gradually relaxed. Afterwards I made tea for everyone with the last of the teabags I had taken from Tammy's stash. We sat in the living room, the TV down low, Lucas laying across Mom's knee.

"You about ready to start back at school, missy?" Mom asked.

I shook my head. "Not quite."

"Alright, you know best. Don't leave it too long now."

My eyes darted over and back in disbelief. Who was this woman? She had more personalities than a hospital had patients.

Lucas raised himself from his relaxation and disappeared for a second before returning with *Farmer Duck*, his bedtime book. He climbed back onto her knee.

"What a great lil boy you are, mister." said Mom. "You ready for bed?" Lucas nodded. "Ok, then."

She licked her fingers and started reading, her smoky southern drawl hypnotic. The book was magic. "Quack, said Farmer Duck as he gathered all the animals. Quack, said Mr. Pig. The hens chuckled."

Maybe things weren't so bad after all. My eyes grew heavier and heavier.

Chapter 2

I woke with a start the following morning when I heard the front door slam and a bunch of cussing. Disoriented, I looked around the room, trying to figure out where I was. I squeezed into my jeans real quick and found Mom standing at the counter sucking a beer from a fresh six pack like she was a toddler ready for bed. She was dressed in jeans and white shirt, and a pair of heels trailed behind her in the hallway. She slammed the bottle down empty, gasping for breath before reaching for another.

"Mom? What happened?" She was like a balloon two weeks after the party, crinkled and deflating.

She sucked her bottom lip in so that her front teeth came forward like a shark's. Then she took a gulp from a second bottle. I moved closer.

"Mom, stop. What's the matter?"

"Oh, it's nothing. It's just the way it is."

I thought about grabbing the beer from her fist, but something told me not to.

"Tell me," I said softly.

She shrieked and released a ton of tension alongside. "I had an interview for a new job today, you know?" Mom always finished her sentences real high and sing-songy. "And well, I was up nice and early. I washed my hair and ironed this here shirt." It was unbuttoned, showing off her cleavage. "I got there plenty early, and

17

you know what that miserable secretary said to me. She says, 'Sorry, ma'am, but the position has been filled'."

"Oh, no," I said.

"She said, 'I'm terrible sorry, but Mr. Hendries was very happy with the first gal who interviewed that morning and offered her the job right then, right there'. And I says, but that ain't right, we all deserves the chance to change his mind, and the secretary said sorry, there was nothing she could do. And she said if any more positions open up, I should apply. But I told her she could shove her positions where the sun don't shine." Mom took a long drink.

"Oh, Mom."

"Well, what you gonna do?" she asked frankly.

"You know you probably oughtn't have said that…I mean, Wendy's pays good. If another job opens, they might not ask you…"

Mom was silent. I exhaled hard. With one long gulp, she finished the bottle and went for another.

"I don't think the beer's gonna help."

"It sure as hell don't make things worse. Don't worry, I'm only gonna have one more and go to bed. Help me sleep and think."

Later I found her in the living room drinking beer and watching some old black and white movie. She was crying quietly and mumbling something about poor Mrs. Dolores. I sat reading opposite for a while wondering if I should say something, fearful that if I tried to spin the situation positive, she would lash out. When her beers were finished she fished out a bottle of brown liquid from some place and poured a mighty glass.

"Mom," I protested.

She looked up at me with such disdain. "What? WHAT?"

I swallowed hard. "That stuff's only gonna make things worse. You can't get sad about one interview. Wait 'til you see. Something will show up."

"Well, isn't that just swell, little miss know-it-all. You'll see what it's like one day, how hard it is to make right all the time. 'Course you too clever to fall into that trap."

A bloodless wave overcame me. It was like I was made of Jell-O as I rose to get out of there. Would Mom ever change her ways?

I went in my room and read the only book I could find that hadn't been scribbled in and colored on, which was *Little Women*, and waited until after three. Then I called Vinnie and told him to meet me in town.

He asked me if I had spoken to Michelle since I got back. Michelle was my closest girl. We used to hang out all the time, the three of us. Last year when we were both a little dumber, we had promised to be each other's bridesmaids, to get married at the same time and to raise our families in Alderhill. Those ideas seemed like fantasy now. Michelle hadn't contacted me since the time I'd left for Cleveland that January; she knew I was back but still hadn't picked up the phone to say hi.

I felt angry about that, and when I said this to Vinnie, he said "Alex, you know Michelle doesn't even own a cell, and she has no interest in Facebook or computers. You didn't call her either when you were gone. She misses you."

When I got off the phone with Vinnie, I called her. "Hi. Listen, I'm sorry we haven't talked."

"Alex! Jeez, I missed you, man. Let's hang out!"

"I'm going to the diner with Vinnie shortly. Wanna come?"

"I'm there!"

I went out to the barn and uncovered my dusty red bike. The back tire was kinda soft and the chain had fallen off, but I soon fixed that. It was a fifteen-minute ride to town, all windy and downhill from our green patch up the mountain. Getting home was no fun. Usually I asked one of the ol' timers at the gas station if I could put my bike in the back of their truck, and they'd drop me home.

It wasn't exactly much of a town either. We didn't really have a main street, just a couple stores—hardware, pharmacy, a bank—all scattered around, with the main flow of traffic by a gas station that was next to the supermarket, which in turn was next to a little old diner. Applebee's was a little farther, just off the interstate.

The three of us met and shared pancakes and coffee. Michelle couldn't get over my pixie cut and took almost five minutes to settle down before we could actually talk. Her hair hadn't changed in years, always in tight braids, but they really suited her cute little face. She wanted to know all about Cleveland.

"Guys, when you go and see another city, you realize just how behind the times things are here. We got nothing here, and the government gives us nothing."

"But it's home, Alex, right?" asked Michelle, breaking a piece of crispy bacon with her fingers and chewing slowly.

I nodded. "I love it here...but home is bad. Guys, I don't know what to do about Mom and Dad. I'm scared for Lucas."

Michelle nodded with pursed lips. Vinnie looked out the window.

"You're not thinking of takin' him and runnin' away?" said Michelle.

My eyebrows made a perfect V. "Noooo! I need to help Mom and Dad."

Vinnie cleared his throat. "I know your ma, Alex. She's always drunk when she's not workin'. You need to help her get back to work. You know, my mom said there's shifts opening at the factory...Those are long ass hours, she wouldn't have time to drink."

"Yeah, that could work. Maybe she just needs a little encouragement," I said.

"Yeah, Alex. You're good with computers. Why don't you type her out something nice she can practice and say when she goes for an interview, just like we did that one time in speech class," said Michelle.

"Yeah, I can do that."

***

That evening I spoke with Mom as she sat watching TV.

"Mom, I was thinking. I can help you get a job." She looked at me, confused. "Vinnie's mom said there were positions opening up at the candy factory. That'd be good, huh?" I sang my sentences this time, trying to make it sound exciting. "I mean, you like candy, don't you?"

Her face mellowed.

"I mean, candy has a certain appeal, I guess."

"Have you got a resume?"

"I got something like one."

"I can help you make up a resume on the computer. Maybe you can dress a little different. Where's that nice skirt you used to wear waitressing at Luigi's? You need something like that and a nice shirt, maybe a scarf too. We should go to Target."

"I guess that sounds nice," she said.

"I'll call Vinnie's mom right now and ask for her boss's number. We'll try and set up an interview. Ok?"

"Ok. I guess. Ok, let's try tomorrow," she said, her smile broadening.

Chapter 3

The following morning, I called the factory. Interviews were taking place the next day, and I was lucky to get Mom's name down in time. Mom showed me her resume, which was handwritten on lined yellow paper and folded more times than the very first piece of origami. I started up the old desktop in the corner of the living room and got to work. Mom brought me a fresh cup of coffee, and we worked for an hour making it look right. She kept asking me dumb questions the whole time.

"How much money you think that Mr. Microsoft has from sellin' all those computers? You know, I learned to type when I was your age. You should learn like I did, would save you a hell of a lot of time, instead of punching all the letters with the same three fingers," she said, nodding intrusively at me.

"What?" I shrieked and somehow managed to stop myself from firing my anger at her. She could have done this all by herself with her magical typing skills.

"And sit up straight too, else your back will be in trouble." She was crouched behind me, breathing her yucky breath into my ear as I typed.

I found myself scratching my cheek real hard where there wasn't even an itch, and my shoulders were getting tense from all the shallow breathing. It was one hell of a long hour.

"How about we go get some stuff at the store. Maybe later we can work on your interview techniques," I said, trying to free up some personal space.

We headed for Target after lunch. Mom had forgotten all about the previous day's failed interview and was excited looking at skirts and heels to match. She wanted this ruby-colored lipstick, but I encouraged her to keep it natural, to let her great personality shine. All the lying and charm was a struggle, but I had to grin and suck it up.

When we got home, we saw Dad with his shirt sleeves rolled up, digging a gutter to release the rain water that made the grass soggy and brown at the bottom of the steps to the trailer. Lucas was gathering the running water into some beer bottles and dumping them in the old well. Dad rested on his shovel and waved as we carried the groceries inside. I was surprised he had taken the concrete lid off the well. Not so long ago, anytime Mom yelled for Lucas and he didn't answer, it would be the first place she'd run to look.

As the day wore on, I felt antsy. Mom hadn't stopped talking since sun-up, and I realized it was the longest amount of time I had spent in her company since I was a baby. I wasn't particularly loving it, but somehow I mustered the patience to finish what I'd started.

"Ok, Mom, let's practice your interview skills."

"Sure thing," she said, walking into the living room with a fresh cup of coffee and flopping onto the couch. I clenched my teeth, then rolled my shoulders and inhaled for five, exhaled for eight. Then I realized I could get my own back a little.

"You can't practice your interview laying back like that, Mom, we gotta do this right. Come on now, into the kitchen."

She made resentful noises but followed.

"Sit back straight now," I said with a wry smile. Her snake eyes kept veering off, and I clicked my fingers to bring her attention back. "Mom, you can't trust nobody who doesn't look you in the eye. Now, where were we?" I made my voice deep. "Ma'am, why didn't you like working as a cook at your last job?"

She sighed and looked up at the static fan not yet warm enough for use.

"What was it like up there by the lake? I bet Tammy thinks she's great livin' up in the burbs with that bearded hosier?"

"Mom, focus!"

"What was it you asked me?"

"Your last job. Why didn't you like it?" I spat.

Mom's face distorted, and she shook her head back and forth. "Oh my, nuh-uh. I just hated having to slice up all that awful meat, especially the chicken. The chicken was the worst, and you know that smell? Anytime I cook chicken now I fry it in so much oil to make sure the smell is gone. Sometimes I won't even eat it."

"Jeez, Mom! I should fire you from this house!"

"I hate that chicken meat, Alex. God knows how they get them breasts so big. You ever see a real chicken? Your grandma used to have them runnin' around; they ain't never had meat on them like they do nowadays!"

I had to go back to square one and explain that an interview was a chance for her to lie and tell everyone how great she was. What I really wanted was to run my frustration into the ground. But Mom was happy to have someone to yap at. She was like a skunk's essence following me around. I needed to finish up quick and escape.

With my skin still crawling and muscles tense, I went for a stroll before dark. I walked up Clover's Hill, watching the sun go down and whistling a little ditty to clear my mind. Harper followed alongside, smiling all the way. I guess Harper used the route every day, 'cause the grass wasn't long like every place else, kind of like a highway for dogs.

When I got home, Mom had baked homemade pizzas with Cajun chicken and peppers and sun-dried tomatoes. Lucas poured the biggest glass of milk, drank half, then couldn't eat dinner.

"It tastes great, but there ain't nowhere in my stomach to put it," he moaned.

I was nervous that Mom would hit up the fridge for a beer during dinner, but thankfully she didn't, although she did seem edgy. The day had been a relative success, and sleep came without surprises.

Chapter 4

Mom came home real positive after her interview the next day. She said the man kept nodding and smiling and she had a real good feeling about it. She started making spaghetti sauce for dinner and kept looking at the phone, hoping it might ring. But soon she was pacing and mumbling and talking in long, jumbled sentences. She smoked one after another of Dad's cigarettes until the place was like an old-time jazz hall. I told her to go outside if she was gonna smoke any more, but she said it was too cold.

"Here," I said, handing her the TV remote. "Try and relax."

Dad also sat, and soon they were arguing about which show to watch. I took the phone into the bedroom and called Lakewood. Tammy answered.

"Hi, Alex. Buck told me you called, and I meant to ring back, but I've been in bed sick every day. How are things now?"

"I'm gonna go with meh. I'm workin' on a plan."

"Ok, good. Did you call your grandpa? You make sure he knows everything that's going on. Make sure you go to his house every day for some rest."

"I will. How's Kate? Is she there?"

"Hold on." She came back a moment later. "I'm afraid she's still sore that you left. She doesn't feel like coming to the phone right now."

"Oh," I said, hurt.

"Don't worry. She'll come 'round. Is there anything we can do for you in the meantime?"

"Um, I guess not."

"Make sure to keep in touch. Take care. Bye."

Bored, I decided to sort out my closet, picking out the shirts that were too small and jeans with tears too big to call fashionable anymore and put them in a trash bag.

Later, we sat down to dinner. Mom made nice conversation but I could tell — I think we all could — that something wasn't right. She asked Dad and I to wash up after dinner and went to the living room with a six pack of beer. I found my breath catching in my chest and felt a little dizzy. It was like the house was too small, like there was only enough oxygen for one or two people and when things weren't running smooth, we were all competing for the same air. I was worried about Mom and what might happen if she didn't get the job. Not feeling so hot, I went outside.

The sun was a big orange ball ready to go to sleep behind our barn. I walked little steps in no particular direction, trying to think. A thought occurred to me. When I was in Lakewood and feeling bad, I'd watched Kate dance. Images of our adventure to State Championships in Cincinnati came flooding back and made me tingle inside. I had never seen a happier face than when Kate had won first prize.

Ballet was my first love, but I had come to love the Irish dancing movements. And I had an idea. I crossed the field to the barn, which was a junk goldmine. Dad had old lawnmowers and bits of rope and an old cement mixer and hay for Roly all scattered here and there. There were bits of carpet and lengths of wood and tools and a sofa and all sorts. The only empty space to actually walk around without tripping over something was in Roly's pen. I heard Dad follow behind, an axe in his hand.

"Dad, c'mere a second." I said as I tried to pull a long sheet of wood from behind some old furniture. "Figure I need a strong man to make me a space."

He came over, scratching his forehead.

"What kind of space?"

"I'm gonna need a sheet or two of this ply, gonna make a place to dance."

"Dance?"

"Yeah, Dad, dance. You remember how Grandma used to do that old Irish?"

"I do," he said fondly.

"Well, I'm learning."

"Good for you!" He grinned at me with his dimpled smile. "Now, I ain't sure that piece gonna be big enough. What you need, four by seven or so?"

"As much as will cover the pen."

"Ok, I'll call Mac, see if he's got any sheeting left over."

Still feeling uneasy, I decided to sweat it out before daylight sunk. I changed into some old clothes and went running. I didn't have any music to make it easier, but I ran up Clover's Hill through the open fields, past our neighbor's house and in through the trees. I wasn't going much more than a brisk walk, and soon that became too much. I turned for home. It was such a pretty picture, the trees golden from a sinking orange fire ball in the distance. My face was sweaty and throbbing. I crawled the final mile home, exhausted, dehydrated and dizzy. I stretched my leg muscles and waited for the sweating to end so as I could take a hot soak in the shower.

I had to make do with thirty seconds under a cold spray. They mustn't have been paying the electricity bills. Soon we'd have no lights. Good thing it was almost summer.

I slept late into the morning and woke tired. Mom was still slumbering. While eating breakfast, I saw Dad's friend Mac drive his truck down our laneway, and with nothing else to do, I went to see what they were up to. I put on Dad's rain jacket after looking at the threatening sky.

Dad and Mac struggled down the muddy slope carrying a large sheet of wood.

"Are you the cause of this inconvenience?" Mac joked, and spat tobacco spit as I followed behind. He always wore a faded tan bucket hat no matter the weather, but guess he had to, 'cause he was bald as an egg.

"Yep, sir."

"You're gonna be a dancer, huh? Well, I say good for you. Dancing's good for the heart. I ain't never seen a dancer who didn't seem to be enjoying themselves."

They spent the next hour laying the boards just right, more than enough sheets to have a few layers, and I figured that would help protect my joints from the concrete underneath. They screwed the pieces nice and firm into place.

Dad smiled when I returned with two cups of coffee. Mac swept away the saw dust, leaving my dance space just perfect. He then handed me the brush.

"Why don't you finish this off, darlin', I got one more thing to get from the truck."

He came back with a full-length piece of mirror that must have been attached to a wardrobe once upon a time. He had a great big grin on his face. When he rested the mirror, I threw down the brush and gave him a hug.

"Jeez, Mac, thanks buddy!"

"My pleasure. I sure don't got any need for lookin' at it."

Soon the boys were out of the way and I was left to marvel at my new 'studio'. The space inside Roly's pen looked amazing. The boys had hung the mirror just right so I could see myself from the center of the floor. They'd even painted the back and side wall a light color cream just to take away the concrete bore. An extension cable ran all across from the power socket at the other side of the barn, hooked up to a cd player. I felt a floaty happiness at that moment and wanted to cry. But instead, I gritted my teeth. "Everything's gonna work out, Alexandra. I promise."

I ran to my bedroom and pulled a black cloth bag from under my bed, shiny velvet on the outside, a kind of plastic inner. I loosened the rope and pulled out the worn, heavy shoes Kate had bought me with money from her own piggy bank. I fingered the soft leather, the hard block heel and worn-down tip, and had to swallow hard. It was weird, but in a way, I hated kindness. I could hear Mom muttering in the kitchen and swallowed. I wasn't going to think about it. Shoe bag under my arm, I marched out to the barn.

I didn't have any Irish music to dance to, so I just did some over two-threes and sidesteps, always remembering what Kate had beaten into me—to keep my feet turned out. I worked and worked on this until my body instinctively knew what to do and I didn't have to look in the mirror to see if it was right any more. Then I practiced rallying, in my sneakers first, then a little with the heavy shoes. I had to go real easy, else I'd break my butt—it had been more than two months since the last time I had tried, under Martin's supervision.

After my body warmed up, I really got into it, hammering as hard as I could, trying to make the floor bounce and push me higher into the air with each stomp. I danced hoping that by not thinking, a solution to the Mom problem might magically appear.

Chapter 5

Several days of insignificance passed with Mom ignoring calls to fill in waiting at Luigi's because it interfered with her drinking and sleeping all day. Dad was pretty idle too, except for fixing odds and ends 'round the house. It made for tense, unpleasant evenings with both slackers slacking. I was beginning to go stir crazy and wanted to start back in school, but the thought of leaving Lucas under Mom's supervision prevented me from doing so.

One midday Vinnie messaged. He had skipped school and wanted me to come over. I wanted to bring Lucas even though I knew Vinnie wouldn't approve. Lucas hadn't been to daycare in months, and that wouldn't change until they both went back working. I went to get him and heard all sorts of hammering and grunting noises coming from the barn.

"What you making, little man?"

"It's a house for birds to live in when it's winter time."

I examined the three pieces of wood he had roughly nailed together in some kind of triangular shape.

"It doesn't really look much like a birdhouse," I said.

"You know what? I changed my mind. It's art. I'm making art."

I nodded. "Sounds about right. Ok, little buddy. Get your bike. We're going to Vinnie's."

"Great," he yelped, and scampered off.

Vinnie lived a couple miles down the hill, not quite as far as the gas station. When we got there, I fetched Lucas some milk and sat him down at Vinnie's Xbox in the living room. Then I quietly opened the door to Vinnie's bedroom, where he lay pretending to be sick.

"Hanging on that there chair," he said sleepily. "My shirt. It's getting too tight. You want it?"

"I love that shirt on you," I whimpered.

"Well, it's yours now."

I tore off my t-shirt and tried on the black and white check shirt, Vinnie watching with a glint in his eye.

"Looks good," he said.

I kneeled by the side of the bed and gave him a kiss on the cheek. Just then we heard a bunch of mumbling at the front door. Vinnie, wearing just his shorts, got up to check.

"What you doing home so early?" he asked.

His mom's little round face was all pale and concerned. She brushed curly strands of auburn from her eyes and rested her hand on her cheek.

"Oh, I got some toothache real bad. And these pills don't get rid of the pain," she said, rattling a box of Aleve. "I can hardly keep my eyes open for the pain."

"Maybe you should see a tooth doctor," said Vinnie.

"Or an optometrist, if it's trouble with your eyes?" I added.

She wasn't sore enough to not give us a funny look. "You didn't think I hadn't thought of that? That's where I'm going shortly."

Lucas kept himself amused while Vinnie and I lay on his bed talking. He refused to shave his fuzzy facial hair, so I refused to kiss him. At five we got hungry and made pasta with tomato sauce and cheese. Vinnie's mom came home shortly after.

"I got me an abscess tooth. Dentist gave me these here antibiotics to kill it," she said before popping the cap and swallowing one without water. She sat down and nibbled on some food, but the spaghetti was too much work for her mouth, so instead she took a big glass of white wine from the fridge. We talked maybe half an hour, but Vinnie's mom became quieter and paler as the minutes passed. She rested her head in her hands, elbows on the table.

"What's the matter Mom?"

"Sheesh, I dunno. Must have been that spaghetti sauce. My head is starting to spin, and my stomach don't feel right."

Vinnie and I looked at each other. "I dunno, Mom, I feel just fine. How 'bout you, Alex?"

"Oh, just fine. Might I suggest a trip to the gastroenterologist?"

I had barely finished my sentence when she got up and ran for the bathroom. She spent the next five minutes throwing up as Vinnie and I tried not to laugh.

Just as darkness set in, Lucas and I cycled home, unsure of what awaited us.

***

I should have known better or at least been more cautious, but tingling with loved-up energy after spending time with my favorite boys, I arrived home a little too happy. Miserable people hated happy people. That was a fact. Mom was chopping carrots and bacon slices.

"Hey Moms, how was your day? See any job adverts in the paper today?" I said, all cheerful. But she didn't answer. "Might be worth checking from time to time, you know?"

Mom growled. "You want me to get a job so bad, why don't you check for me. Or better still, you old enough, how about you look for your own self?"

And like that, a new old routine developed. She'd drink to get drunk and become unbearable. I started to keep well out of sight, but Lucas wasn't smart enough to do that. A couple times he came to me struggling for breath, his asthma real bad, and it was always after Mom had scolded him for nothing other than what you'd expect four-year-old boys to get up to. I spent most evenings at Vinnie's or Michelle's but felt guilty about leaving Lucas behind.

As the days rolled by, I used my new dance space to the max. It was an area of calm and distraction. At the beginning, my fitness was so bad I could only manage twenty minutes before almost dying of exhaustion, but a little running every day helped.

There was an old clock above the barn door. I would practice the beginner reel over and over, trying to leap higher and point sharper with every movement. I watched closely in the mirror and corrected myself. It was taking a real effort to make sure my arms stayed by my sides as I danced. I refused to look at the clock until I couldn't take it anymore. Soon I would need harder steps to dance.

One night Mom was in a real humor. As we sat down to eat, Dad tried making nice.

"Debby, bet you didn't know Alex has a new hobby?"

"She does?"

"Yes, sir. Irish dance," he said, winking at me.

She raised her eyebrows. "Good grief, that's something. Ain't you a little old for that?"

I stopped chewing but didn't take the bait.

"I mean, I guess humans is never too old to learn," she continued. "But guess I don't see the point."

"You don't think it's nice she found something she enjoys?" asked Dad.

She shook her head real stubborn. "No, no, I do not. There ain't no point in wasting time with something that's never gonna make no difference to nothing."

Mom kept on in that vein, and I blocked out the words. Dad became aggrieved and stuck up for me, the two of them getting redder in the face. I wasn't hungry anymore, so I left my plate by the sink, grabbed Lucas and my dance gear and headed for the barn. Lucas rode around on his big wheel as I danced. Even though the exercise helped, I felt very much on edge most of the time.

"Well, look at you shakin' that ass," a voice called, and I stopped abruptly. It was Vinnie, with a big smile on his face.

"Don't stop on account of me. I'm impressed with my barn-dancing girl."

He came over and kissed me. I sighed.

"What's the matter?"

"Momma's drinking, and they won't stop fighting. Vinnie, I'm worried."

"Right." He stepped back and folded his arms. "What set it off this time?"

"Nothing special."

"Did you try talking to her? Does she see clear the day after? Isn't she feeling sick?"

I shook my head. "She doesn't do hangovers."

"What you mean?"

At that moment, the front door of the house swung open and Mom shouted, "Go on now. Get outta here!"

Vinnie and I peeped round the barn door. Mom dumped a bottle of beer into her mouth, then threw it after the yelping dog.

Vinnie must have seen how sad I was, because he just grabbed me and held me tight.

"Ok, I gotta go. I'll be back later. I have an idea. Just keep it cool now."

Vinnie took off on his bike, and I stared blankly at my dance floor. Not five minutes later, Dad rushed out of the house, threw something in the trunk of his car and sped off. I wondered if he had finally given up on Mom, on us.

There was no point going back inside, so I continued dancing until I was tired enough to face her. I knew then it was imperative I went back to school. But I didn't like to leave Lucas with her, as terrible as it was to think that she would do anything bad. I figured she didn't have to do anything especially bad; just acting the way she did around him was plenty bad enough. It was becoming more and more important on so many levels to get him back into daycare.

I took Lucas with me into the bedroom early that night to stay out of harm's way. I listened to the scratching of coloring pencils on paper and Lucas's gentle self-talk but couldn't relax, checking my phone every five minutes waiting for Vinnie to call or message. Just as my eyes grew heavy enough for slumber, I heard a gentle tap-tap at my window. I recognized the silhouette right away and crept out of bed, Lucas fast asleep. A warm May breeze carried Vinnie's manly smell through the open window.

"Here," he said, stretching out his arm. He handed me three large white pills. I looked up wide-eyed and shrugged. "They're for your mom."

"Huh?"

"Remember my mom had that toothache? Remember how she started getting sick? These pills are called Flagyl or something. You cannot under any circumstances drink alcohol when you take these pills," he whispered excitedly, the moonlight reflecting the glint in his eyes. "Mom was spitting puke every twenty minutes after drinking wine that time. It happened a second time too, until she read the instructions."

"Are you serious? You want me to poison Mom? Are you crazy?"

He smiled. Mom was bad, but this was extreme. This was not me. Vinnie pressed my hand until it formed a fist around the pills. I wondered if Dad had come home.

"But Vinnie," I tried again, whispering urgently, "I can't...Your mom—"

"What about my mom?"

My brain searched for a response. "Em, your mom...she needs these..."

"Her tooth is fine now."

"No. You don't understand. Doctors always say you need to complete the course."

Lucas stirred a little in his bed, but I kept going with a quieter whisper.

"Doctors always say..." I changed my voice and tightened the shape of my mouth, and the words came out all gentlemanly. "Now make sure you finish the course even if your symptoms have gone; it's the only way to be sure the infection has been killed, otherwise it could come back worse than ever."

Vinnie rolled his eyes and turned to leave. "This was a second box they gave her and she didn't need 'em in the end." He paused. "Alex, if you ain't gonna fix your life, hell, poison your own self for all I care, at least it'll put you out of your misery."

His eyes smiled. He was always gonna be trouble. Just as I thought he was about to leave, he pulled the top half of his body through the window, grabbed my head and kissed me hard, biting my lip. Then he swept his sandy hair from his eyes and left without a goodbye.

I felt so angry with him and lay in bed mulling over everything. The idea was sick—literally. Was I the kind of person to do something like that, and if so, was that ok with me? Something had to give. But what? There had to be another way.

Chapter 6

The next day I felt so depressed that even dancing didn't have its usual effect. It felt like my intestines were tangled and contracting tightly inside my stomach, and it was almost impossible to breathe right. I was so weak and light-headed, all I could do was watch TV.

Lucas had taken some bedsheets from the linen closet and made a tent in the living room using the sofa in the middle of the room and some kitchen chairs. It spanned across to the kitchen door, which made it awkward to pass through. He dragged a box of toys and books from our bedroom in there. I tried to relax with the TV low and Lucas talking quietly to his action figures.

Soon Dad called us for dinner. We sat down to eat his famous mac and cheese, which he ate straight from the pot. Mom came into the kitchen, slobbering her words, and made straight for me with her eyes.

"Hey, little miss prissy. Where's my dinner? You didn't make your own momma dinner?"

I looked at her innocently, palms upturned. "I...I didn't know. I didn't make dinner."

"Come on now, Debby, settle down," said Dad. "I asked you five times, and you didn't answer."

"Don't you start, you good-for-nothing bum."

Dad mumbled something about getting washed up. I stopped chewing, my stomach doing that thing again with the guts ringing themselves like a wet sponge. I gripped the corner of the table as Dad left the kitchen, Mom scurrying after, itching for more confrontation.

"What in the hell is all this? My good sheets. I'll kill him."

Mom came running back into the kitchen, white linen dragging behind, a look of ferocity shining at Lucas, whose face was whiter than white. I sucked like a fish for air, close to fainting. There had been another time I'd felt this bad—the time I'd run away in Lakewood and taken the bus heading home. I'd hoped to never feel that fear again, the feeling that my passing was imminent, but it was back. Somehow, somewhere, a nervous energy rescued me.

"Did you do this? What in heaven's name were you thinking? You don't think your momma has enough to worry about...Put out those hands 'til I show you what happens to bad boys like you."

I rose quickly, knocking over my chair, and lifted Lucas right out of there. He was too scared to cry. Mom came after us but stumbled over the sheets she had trailing behind her, which bought me enough time. I pushed the wardrobe up against the bedroom door as she came a hammering. But then Dad came.

"Come on Debby, he was just playing is all."

But Mom started shouting. Lucas held his hands to his ears. With some quick thinking, I spotted my cd player, switched on the radio and turned the sound up loud. Lucas wheezed and wheezed, his face gray. I fished his inhaler out of the end table, and he took a puff from the almost empty blue tube. I took a puff also to see if it would help me. I held him close until finally the wheezing eased.

After an hour, I felt I needed some air. I climbed out the bedroom window and walked a little; the fireflies were lighting up and dying out in the dark. They lit up with a moment's short-lived inspiration then disappeared, never fluorescent long enough to show me the way. My forehead was clammy. I sighed slow and hard through my nose. I had no choice.

After that, it was all about timing. I observed Mom's movements through the living room window from outside and bided my time. She was relaxing, if you could call it that, with some beers.

I waited until she finally went to the bathroom. I took my pre-crushed pills, carefully sieved it into the half-empty beer can on the coffee table and swirled it around—almost too much, because it started to foam. I didn't have time to wait around and see what would happen, as I heard the bathroom door unlock. It was time to hide and wait.

***

That night I lay in bed listening to Mom coughing and hacking every twenty minutes asking myself just what I had done. The guilt ate through me and only stopped when fear came to take its place. What if I'd poisoned her too much? What if something terrible happened? How could I ever live with myself? After Mom's fourth trip to the bathroom, her stomach must have settled, and the house became still. I slept, although it was not restful.

The following day, Mom lay green-faced on the couch. I felt awful. Dad had gone to work. I helped Mom into bed and brought her coffee, which she couldn't drink. She was burning up. I finally got her to drink some water, but it was as if she had been struck on the head with a bat. She could not keep her eyes open.

Mom spent another three days in bed with fever-like symptoms. At one point, she yelled out like crazy in the middle of the day, and I found her tossing around, possessed, shivering but on fire, her nightgown and bedsheets soaking. I opened a window to let the cool air in, placed a wet towel on her head and made her drink some water. Mom was an addict, and I didn't know why or what it was about life that forced her to drink. And I hoped beyond hope that somehow this punishment would help her come out of it better.

All weekend I kept an eye on the household. I made soup with the scraps left in the fridge—some carrot ends, yellowing broccoli, an onion and bits of bacon to give the broth some taste. I danced lots more and thought about Kate. I called again, but she was out. I told Tammy to tell her I had fixed up a place in the barn so I could practice.

Mom was still unwell after the weekend, so I stayed off school to mind Lucas. I did some writing with him— showed him how to hold a pencil and form letters and numbers and whatnot. We then snuggled on the couch and watched movies.

By Wednesday evening, Mom was out of bed. She looked totally different. Her face looked fresh and her skin not as flaked. That's when I realized she had gone almost seven full days without a drink, which was probably the first time that had ever happened.

Lucas didn't know how to react. She picked him up and brought him to the sofa and rested him across her lap, stroking his head. I think he liked it, but I didn't know how to deal with it. Dad didn't take any notice. His face was cement-gray despite washing umpteen times. He looked tired but content. That was until he opened the fridge and saw there wasn't a pick of food.

"Jeez, Alex," he mockingly groaned. "What kinda homestead you keeping here? You expect that strong boy down the street to come a-calling on you for marriage? You better buck up your ideas, missy."

Even though I knew he was jesting, I still took the bait.

"God damn, Pa. I've been here all week doing nothing but chores, and I may as well be fishing the swamp for food. You didn't leave us any money. I'm like one of those women in Africa walking all those miles just to bring back a jug of water. Why don't you let me drive already?"

There must have been smoke coming out of my ears. Lucas watched tentatively from behind the couch, not sure if the yelling was real or playful, but Mom was smiling, especially after Dad made little dancing motions upsides his face as I spoke.

"Well, what's a man to do?" he pondered. Then he dug his hands in his back pocket and produced a wad of cash. "Ain't it good that some people work around here so they can treat their loved ones to some Mexicano? I don't know 'bout you guys, but I'm starved. Scrub up and in the car in fifteen. We're going to Tonto's 4 Taco's!"

And so it was. Dad drove us a thirty-minute ride to the best burrito house in Kentucky. It was run by a family of el Mexicans who had basically opened up their kitchen and living area for people to come and eat. They had one guy suited and booted all in white, making cocktails. Then three other guys with black suits and sombreros strolled around strumming guitars and singing.

Dad told us stories of the practical jokes he and Mac had played on their site manager. I got a little worried when he ordered a margarita and Mom a beer but soon as she drank half the bottle, she started turning off-white. She went to the bathroom and came back wiping her mouth, breathing deep.

Things didn't get any easier for Mom, though. She mustn't have realized what she'd ordered was full of jalapenos. Her face turned redder than a bee-stung butt, and we sat there laughing at her.

The food was so good. I had tacos filled with sizzling strips of beef, sour cream and cheese. Lucas loved the sweet-potato fries. Dad had two long drinks and that was it.

"I don't want no more. I gotta drive, and besides I have to break my ass on site again tomorrow."

On Sunday night, I heard Mom and Dad discuss Lucas's daycare situation. On Monday morning, I went with Dad to a place in Graysmith, the next town over. Dad had mixed feelings about paying upfront, his wallet an awful lot lighter than before.

"Time for you to go back to school, Alex, and for us to get on with livin' normal," he said when he dropped me home before heading to work.

On Monday evening, Mom got a phone call, and Applebee's offered her her old job back. She bounced around the house singing and even gave me a big squeeze. "Oh my, Alex. It's so good to have you back. Things just aren't the same when you're not around. I mean, you're always kickin our butts, but you mean right." She smiled.

Everything was beginning to work out better than ever. I was finally making a difference and helping my family. For once I felt positive that everything would be ok, and it was time to focus on me and what I wanted from my life.

Chapter 7

I went back to school the second Monday in May. The teachers didn't recognize me on account of my hair being so short and because of my test scores. Mr. Lind gave us a math refresher test, and after correcting, had the zip to say "Alexandra, you're like Samson, except the opposite. I think you should keep that new hairstyle."

Everything was better than ever. Dad was working all the time, and Mom was on a couple shifts a week. One Saturday after Mom had finished her lunch shift, she came home and took Lucas and I to the mall. It was like Christmas Day—we were each allowed any two things we wanted, within reason. I got new jeans and a shirt. Mom and I drank coffee and talked about a summer vacation. She was sad that we'd missed out on the Kentucky Derby. She really loved it at the track.

Every weekend Mom would let me do the grocery shopping while she and her friend Dorothy had coffee. I picked out some vegetables and good meats, trying to go the healthy route.

Lucas loved daycare. He sucked up whatever they taught him and repeated it to us every night. I studied hard. Summer exams were the second week in June and I really wanted aces. I danced every day and loved how it made me feel. It also helped my brain concentrate when it was time to study.

Vinnie and I were more in love than ever. One day he cycled to my house with a crumpled bunch of colorful flowers he must have picked in the fields by his house. I gave him a soft kiss as we sat beneath the chestnut tree for shade.

"I cannot believe how great everything is. We did it, Vinnie," I said, holding my hand up for a high-five and smiling triumphantly.

He made this face like a Scream mask but didn't keep me hanging.

"Hey, what's that for?"

"Oh, nothing," he said, regretful of his action. "No seriously, you're right. Everything's great. Nice job."

"Buuuuut?"

"I dunno, Alex, just…" He shrugged sheepishly. "Just we been here before, that's all."

But Vinnie was wrong. I was convinced we had all turned down a new road.

I called Lakewood one day. Tammy levelled with me about Kate's operation. She was really struggling with pain and life on crutches, being the hyper type. When I thought back to that day, Kate lying on the stage with her leg at a weird angle, I must have known it wasn't good. I guess I had blocked out those thoughts. When Tammy whispered to Kate that I had been dancing lots, she finally got over her anger and grabbed the phone.

"Alex, you gotta tell me all about your Irish dancing," she squealed.

Kate told me that her idol was coming to Cleveland in July to give Irish dancing workshops. This guy, Kal McGettigan, was the star dancer in *Passion of The Dance*, a show that toured the world. I remembered seeing pictures of the show in Kate's dancing magazines before.

Kal had fallen out with the show's producers and was setting up his own dance company. He had just starred in an Irish dancing reality TV show in Ireland called *Reel Rebels,* and the eight-part series was a total success. A twenty-five-year-old called Kim O' Sullivan who had never competed had won. I was intrigued.

Kate said that everyone on Instagram and Facebook were saying that Kal was working on a new production. Kate really wanted to go to his workshops but said her stupid leg wouldn't be ready in time, as if it was a drumstick cooking slowly in an oven. Kate rambled on and on, but I got distracted, my brain caught in a vicious fantasy, imagining this hot guy teaching me and a bunch of cool kids Irish dance. My fantasy fast-forwarded to Broadway, dancing on stage with thousands of people screaming my name. I was such an idiot.

"When is this workshop? Does it cost like a brief-case load of cash?"

"It's at the start of July. There's a free morning session for beginners."

"Free? Cool. I can afford that."

"There will be tons of babies there. The full weekend is like three hundred dollars. You have to be an Open dancer though. Kal's probably putting together a list of dancers for his new show." My heart fluttered when Kate said that. "Oh my gosh, Alex. You should come. Oh my gosh, come and bring Lucas."

Kate put down the phone and yelled.

"MOM? Mom guess what? Alex and Lucas are coming."

"Wait, Kate, I didn't say…" But she wasn't listening.

Tammy picked up the phone. Kate was babbling by her side.

"Hi, Tam."

"That would be nice if you and Lucas came for a few days."

I glanced into the living room at that moment. Lucas was sitting cross-legged, poking the iPad, Dad was reading a fishing magazine and Mom was sipping coffee and watching TV. "Gosh, I don't know, Tam. Guess things are pretty good here now."

Later I thought real hard about what I wanted from my life. Everything was pretty much bliss. There was really nothing I wanted. I loved school and hanging out with Vinnie and Michelle. It was the definition of contentment. The one thing I did want more of was Irish dancing, and there was a buzz of electricity flowing through my body after talking to Kate.

It felt like I was hallucinating as I walked around outside trying to cool my thoughts, which were filled with luminous images of me performing real good at the Irish dance classes and standing on a stage in my white dress and black tights, bowing to an adoring crowd, red,

red roses landing at my feet. I couldn't shake the adrenaline. Hyperactive, I changed into my dance clothes and went pounding my dance floor in the barn.

Chapter 8

I couldn't get the ludicrous idea of Kal McGettigan's workshops out of my head, so the following day, I made a plan. One way or another, I'd have to learn new steps and needed a teacher. At the school library, I googled a whole bunch of Irish dance stuff. The nearest class was miles away. Luckily, I found lots of clips of dancers teaching material on YouTube, and I settled on this one girl called Melissa Reid's channel. She was maybe twenty-one and had a bunch of reasonably produced vids. She explained that starting off, a beginner needed a reel, light jig, single jig, slip jig, treble jig and hornpipe. I recorded her clips straight onto my phone. I knew the quality wouldn't be the greatest, but it was a start.

Then I made myself a timetable. Starting with the primary reel, I watched it over and over until memorized, then practiced for an hour. Later I did the same except with the treble jig, and soon it was like a compulsion. Every day after school, I was dancing two or three hours, until I no longer needed to watch the vids and my legs knew exactly what to do. It was cathartic.

Life was going great, but one morning coming into June, I noticed something was a little different as I left for school. Mom hadn't been drinking. She had this routine before working a lunch shift—coffee, toasted bagel, radio, yesterday's newspaper, porch, read. But this morning, she sat at the table listless, sipping coffee, caffeine having no effect.

When I got home, she was in bed.

"What's the matter, Mom? You got a migraine?"

She shook her head no. "I don't feel like doing much."

She didn't eat dinner with us that night, and my stomach felt sick as bad thoughts bombarded my brain.

Mom went to work the next day, and that night she seemed both restless and exhausted. She got up and sat down a thousand times before finally grabbing a bottle of beer. I tried to do my homework sitting on the couch opposite, but my concentration was gone, so I went and danced instead. By Thursday, Debby was done. She arrived home from work, pale and sweaty, a paper bag clinking under her right arm.

"Workin' is for idiots," she exclaimed.

"Aw, Mom, maybe it's worse some days, but it ain't that bad, is it?"

"If you think ten hours hard work on minimum wage ain't that bad, well, you're wrong. I'm tired as hell."

"Maybe if you didn't drink beer the night before, you'd be fresher?"

"Oh, is that so? Maybe you're right and maybe you're wrong. You know, one percent of the population owns all the money on this here earth. We are nothing but slaves to help rich white men get richer. If this system ain't the unfairest, rigged nonsense...And you think you're smart, but you're not. You're dumb. Dumber than me, and that's sayin' something."

I got out of there as she kept talking garbage and insults. My gut told me to run. I went outside for some air. Night had yet to fall.

When the weekend came, Dad went to a bar in town with Mac and some friends. Mom bought more beers at the store. I tried to dissuade her.

"Mom, if you're feeling down, why don't you go for a walk or go visit Dorothy or something."

"Oh, Alex, what's the point? Besides, I'm only gonna have one or two. I'm thirsty, and it's humid as hell in here. Besides, why's it ok for your pa to go into town rummaging around skirt like it's a car boot sale and I gotta stay here?"

She dropped a few bottles down her throat and played the radio kind of loud, and I went in the bedroom with Lucas and tried to read.

Later I went to see what she was doing. She was waltzing a beer to some old song, cigarette hanging out of her mouth. When she took a puff, she would sing some of the lyrics, and her voice was real nice and she sang along perfectly. "*Sweet dreams 'til sunbeams find you, sweet dreams that leave your worries behind you,*" and when I saw her blotched eyes, my heart broke.

Our lives were almost perfect, and I couldn't understand why Mom was so unhappy. I went back to bed and couldn't help myself; as the lyrics trickled in through the space between the floor and the door's end, Mom replaying the song over and over, I cried until my pillow was wet. To dream a little dream for Mom.

***

Mom didn't go to work that next week and settled into a more somber state of drunkenness. A couple times as she made her trip to the fridge, I tried to talk her out of it. I tried to remind her how happy she had been the past few weeks, that what she was doing wasn't any good for any of us, but my words went unheard.

One night Dad came home late and sat on the porch sipping a beer. He told me the job he was working on had finished and it looked like construction was slowing down for the time being. I held my breath. Had I really thought things could work out like in the story books? I felt my cheeks burn with embarrassed realization. My gut that told me there weren't many more things I could do to keep our home in order and that the bad old times were about to return. Worst of all, with school being out, I would be idle at home at the nucleus of the warhead. Despite the rolling green fields and rivers reaching wider and farther than my eyes could see, I felt trapped. The storm would move in quick.

Chapter 9

On the first day of school summer vacation, I cried. A guy named Seth in my class was having a house party. Vinnie, Michelle and I went along, and no matter how hard I tried to have a good time and forget about things, I couldn't.

The following days at home were long and restless. Neither Mom nor Dad were working, and the long nights meant more evening time for drinking on the porch and getting feisty. I set up camp in the barn, dancing and figuring things out. I was dancing up to four hours a day. I knew all the beginner dances inside out and was pretty sure everything was on fleek. It was almost time to download a new set of dances from YouTube.

Despite my best efforts to avoid Mom, she came to the barn one day and asked me to put color in her hair. She set a chair outside on the grass, where the set shone down a perfect 78-degree heat.

I set about mixing the color and finding a brush to paint it in, wanting to get it done and be out of there fast as possible. Mom had settled on a disgusting black/purple color, stating that dirty blonde was for bimbos. I bit my lip. My hair was just about to pass my ears and was straw-colored from the sun. I got to work as she sat there smoking and talking garbage.

"Ouch, you're twisting my hair. Can't you do nothing right?"

I tugged the next strand harder.

"You'd never even make a good hairdresser. What kind of daughter I raise you to be with all fingers and thumbs like that?" She took a sip from her bottle.

"I'm trying my best. Keep still."

"Girl, if you wanna make something of yourself, you're gonna need a trade, something you're good at. I guess you can make good chicken; maybe you can be a cook or a waitress or something."

"But Mom, I do well in school. I might go to college."

"College? What you want to do that for? College is just money. It costs a lot of money, and you just putting your life in debt and will never be able to repay the government none of it. That's how they get you. Put you in big debt nice and young, then you a slave to the system. You got good cooking, girl, so you can probably get a good job when you're seventeen. Only thing cookin' is good for is waiting tables and when you're married, but you don't wanna get married, nuh-uh, no way. Unless he's rich, and I mean rich. Then you do whatever he says, and you'll do just fine."

Then she turned 'round and looked at me square.

"If you wasn't so skinny and your butt wasn't so flat and your chest grew something like mine, you'd be real pretty."

"Jesus, Mom, I'm only fifteen. Why you gotta be so mean?"

"You'd be real pretty," she continued. "You could have yourself a rich man for a while. But we got to do something about your mouth. Only contempt comes out of it."

I screeched, not able to take it anymore, and flung the paint brush at the back of her head.

"Ow!" she cried.

"Finish it yourself." I stormed down the hill to where there was a large rock and sat there pondering.

After that, I spent lots of time in Vinnie's. Most times I'd bring Lucas and he'd watch TV or play video games or we'd hitch a ride into town and get ice creams and kick around. I hated summer vacay, having all this time to worry and be idle.

Mom was in a rut and not for shaking, and I was all out of ideas. And Dad didn't help none either. He started making himself scarce and was volunteering at the army base at Fort Knox, training recruits. I danced more and more every day to keep my mind right and bring some order to the disorder, but I felt sick in my brain. One day I told Michelle about my symptoms, how it was hard to breathe and everything, and I thought she would say something dumb, like maybe I had lung cancer, but she said something that frightened me even more.

"You know that kid Donna Jackson? She used to be in our seventh grade? But then she was like gone a year and now she's back redoing her freshman year?"

I shook my head, not really remembering.

"Well, someone told me she had something like what you're saying and she ended up getting all this therapy, and they made her take antidepressants, and you know what, I think she feels fine now. Maybe you need some of those things to help you relax?"

"No freaking way, Michelle," I said, my eyes almost popping out of my skull.

"I mean, if it helps, what's the big deal, right?"

I thought long and hard about what she'd said. Maybe she was right, but as far as I was concerned, the only real long-term cure was anti-Mom pills.

Chapter 10

On the Fourth of July, Dad drove us to Roxboro. We ate at a restaurant with a large terraced seating area that was real nice, except we could only get a table inside. I had a fancy burger and shoestring fries that came in a metal boot. A country band played on a little stage outside. After, we grabbed our picnic blanket and joined the rest of the townsfolk in the park for the fireworks display.

Dancing violet and pink dragons, blue and yellow spaceships and dragons and eagles exploded in the sky, and everyone smiled and cheered and laughed. It felt momentarily wonderful, especially watching Mom huddled against Dad's legs.

But it wasn't lasting. Dad checked his phone two or three times, and Mom drank a few more bottles of beer, and her contented look changed. We left just before midnight, and Lucas slept all the way home despite Mom and Dad bickering the whole way. Soon as we got out of the car, Dad quick marched inside, and Mom started with her loud poison. I was sure the neighbors a half-mile down the mountain would assume the worst and call for help. I carried Lucas into the bedroom and pulled the covers over us without undressing. He buried his head into the small of my back as objects started flying in the kitchen. I lay wide-eyed, biting my lower lip.

"Alex, I promise I'm not gonna cry," he whimpered.

"There's no need to cry. It will be over soon. Just like the other times."

I wished I believed my words. We lay quietly for another few minutes until all of a sudden Lucas dug his nails into my back as a window smashed.

Lucas started to cry. I leapt out of bed. "Stay there, little buddy, I'll be right back."

"Don't, Alex. Stay with me."

My heart was pumping in overdrive as I crept out to the kitchen, wondering what I'd find. Mom was pressing her shoulder against the front door. Dad's bloodied hand was sticking through a broken window panel, where he must have been trying to unlock the door from the outside. He was squealing like a pig with a slit throat. Mom pushed the door back with all her might, her feet sliding under the glass, crunching and grating on the tiles.

"Ow, my hand. Open the goddamned door, you psychopath," Dad yelled.

"You ain't getting back in here."

"I can't get my arm out."

I knew that trying to intervene would end badly. I stepped quickly into the living room and found the phone and dialed Grandpa's number. It rang and rang and finally rang out.

"Come on, Grandpa. Pick it up," I mumbled, re-dialing. When he didn't answer a second time, I called the cops.

"Alderhill County, how may I help?" a lady answered.

"Um, domestic disturbance," I panted.

"What seems to be the problem, ma'am?"

"My mom and dad. They're fighting. There's blood." I could hardly get my words out, and in a strange fortunate way, I knew the lady believed me 'cause she could hear the shouting on her end.

"What's your address?"

"Mountain Rise Road. The house at the very top."

The cop spoke to her partner.

"Mountain Rise, Lieutenant. The house up top." They swapped a few more words before she returned to me. "Ma'am? What's your name?"

"Alex Maslow."

"Ok, Miss Maslow, we're sending a car. Hold tight now."

I went back in the bedroom. Lucas's white eyes lit the room. He sat on the bed, hugging his knees.

"It'll be ok, it'll be ok," I whispered. No more than two minutes later, I heard a third voice. I got up and listened from the kitchen door.

It was Grandpa. The altercation seemed to have ended. Grandpa spied me from behind the door and made a gesture with his chin. I went in the bedroom.

"Quick, Lucas. Let's go."

"Go where?"

"Quick, come on. Don't ask questions this time."

I ushered him out the back door. Mom saw us heading for Grandpa's station wagon as Grandpa met us out front.

"Where d'you think you're taking my kids?"

Grandpa must have been out of breath with anger, 'cause he just pointed at Mom and sucked air trying to muster words, his long gray hair shining silver in the moonlight.

"Deborah. This is…This is the…This is the last of your nonsense!"

Mom came chasing and hollering toward us, but luckily, Dad caught her and winced hard as he held her back. She bucked like a mule and turned the sky blue cussing. Grandpa drove on, wheezing the whole way to his house. Lucas didn't say a word. I took him inside and lay him on Grandpa's sofa and pulled the woolen throw around him. I kissed his freezing forehead. "Relax. It's ok now. I'll be right back, just wanna check on Grandpa."

Grandpa was still in the car, engine running. I prepared a pot of coffee, and by the time he came, inside it was just right. I handed him a cup.

"My sister, Peggy," he started. "Well, she was a real so-and-so, and we fought like cats and dogs." He looked at me with the same pale-blue eyes I had inherited. For the first time, I noticed how wrinkled the skin around his forehead and eyes was. "But we was kids. We fought when we was young-ins. That's no way for grown-ups to act. That's no way for parents…"

You can tell when someone is too old to form tears.

"Can't we call social services? We need to put Mom's ass in jail."

"Please, Alex, don't say that about your mother." There was a pause. "Those two have always been a bad match. I talked with the Child Protection people, but it's a waste of time. She's no good, but believe me, there's worse out there. Those services are stretched beyond capacity, and in their eyes, any kind of re-homing is last resort. The bad things that have to happen for something to change are real bad."

I didn't even feel like crying. At that point, I knew what heaven was. Heaven was a place with an absence of pain. I lay on Grandpa's two-seater sofa next to Lucas, so numb I had no problem sleeping. The following day, I sat out in Grandpa's yard in the sun in a daze.

Dad came later in the afternoon. He and Grandpa talked out front for almost an hour. He then came to talk to me. He put a bunch of twenties in my hand.

"I'm so sorry about this, Alex. I'm bringing your mother to the doctor's, and we're going to fix all this. I want you to call your Aunt Tammy, and you and Lucas are gonna go to Lakewood for some R'n'R, ok?"

I nodded blankly as his puffy eyes tried to smile at me, and he rested his good hand on the back of my head. Then he kissed me on the cheek and went to say bye to Lucas.

I poured myself a glass of cherry juice from Grandpa's narrow fridge and sat at the breakfast bar that

separated the living room from the kitchen. Both ends of
the house looked out through double doors, the
backyard one end and the patio the other.

I dialed the Buckmans' number. Grandpa had an old
black phone with a twist-around dial. It looked good, but
it was a piece of junk.

"Hello?" Buck answered.

"Hi, it's me."

"Oh, hi, Alex. How do? That southern drawl is twice
as smart as last time."

"Yup, reckon so." I smiled into the phone but didn't
know what to say next. The silence only hung for a
moment, because Buck jumped right ahead.

"You know, Tammy and I were hoping you would
come for a visit. We are a little busy today and
tomorrow, but you could come Thursday?"

"Great. That will be good. Can I bring Lucas?"

"Of course."

"Ok, well, guess see you in a couple."

"Bye."

The hinges of the front door shrieked, and Grandpa
entered, out of breath just from climbing the porch steps.

"Grandpa, we got some stuffs to organize."

He nodded dejectedly. But I smiled. There was a
positive from every negative. The weekend in Cleveland
was the weekend of the dance masterclass. I'd make sure
to pack my shoes just in case.

We stayed with Grandpa a couple days and only
went back to the trailer to pack a bag. Early, early

Thursday, Grandpa brought us to the bus stop, both Lucas and I excited to get the heck out of Dodge for a couple days.

Chapter 11

Lucas was like a terrier on the bus looking this way and that. I let him go explore, hoping he'd eventually settle down.

"Alex, this place is a miracle. It even has a potty!" he said as he got back. "The water is a special blue."

He showed me his bleached finger.

"Ew, Lucas. Go wash your hands three times immediately."

He went tromping down the aisle singing a song, his finger in the air. The driver kept glancing in his mirror. When Lucas hadn't returned after a few minutes, I went to check. He was sitting next to an elderly lady.

"Come on, Lucas."

"This ol' lady dropped her scarf, so I gave it back to her."

"Lucas! It's not nice to call someone old…"

"She's seventy-four," he said, matter-of-fact. The lady and her wrinkled face smiled kindly.

Next thing Lucas took a loud bite of the reddest apple I'd ever seen.

"You're not supposed to take things from strangers!"

"She's not a stranger," he said, chewing with his mouth open. "Agnes gave it to me. It's fruit. Didn't you tell me afore kidnappers give you candy? This is fruit, Alex. Fruit!" he said defiantly. "Besides, where's she gonna kidnap me to? We're on the bus for the next four hours, like you said!"

I pursed my lips. "Sorry for disturbing you, Agnes," I said, taking Lucas's hand and dragging him behind.

"He's just darling," she said in an uneven voice. "You're a very lucky mother."

That only resonated with me when I sat down. Mother? Dumb ol' bat! How dare she! I grabbed Lucas's apple, slid the window up top open and threw it out.

"Hey, that was juicy."

"It may have had poison." Lucas's eyes froze.

"Best way to make sure is to rest your head on my lap. Poison doesn't enter the bloodstream when a little boy is lying down."

He went down like a shot. I stroked his hair, and soon we were both asleep. We didn't wake until we reached our stopping point in Cincinnati, both of us glad to stretch our legs.

The second leg of the journey dragged, but finally we got off the bus, and Old Buck greeted us at the station in downtown Cleveland. He had trimmed his beard, which made him much less bear-like. He picked me up and swung me round.

"You don't smell like pipe tobacco anymore," I said.

"I quit, except for special occasions," he said deeply. Then he knelt down on one knee and shook Lucas's hand.

"Who's this brave little chieftain?"

"My name is Lucas," he said, squirming in his little red flip-flops, staring at the ground. He glanced at me, and I said "Go on," and he stretched out and shook Buck's hand before retreating and gripping mine. He looked so cute at that moment I just wanted to die—little blonde cub and the former bear-man.

We got in Buck's battered pick-up truck and made our way to Lakewood.

Lucas couldn't get over the skyscrapers as we drove through the streets of Cleveland. The city was bustling with folk coming and going from bars and restaurants. It looked so full of life and possibility. We passed the ocean-sized lake on the way, a giant light shining from above, which made it feel like daytime. We passed a stretch of beach where a bunch of people listened to a band on a big outdoor stage. Buck rolled down the window, and warm air frazzled my hair. Reggae music spilled into the car briefly, and it felt so relaxing.

Buck parked 'round the back of the house, and I entered through the kitchen. Tammy, sitting at the table reading, took off her glasses and embraced me warmly. She then held me by the shoulders and looked at me real sad.

"Great to see you, Alex." She had cut her hair to her neck. It looked nice, except her roots were graying, which made her look old.

Lucas and Buck followed after with our bags.

"My, who is this handsome man?" asked Tammy.

"My name's Lucas. Tomorrow Buck and I are going to clean up the yard. Here's a gift from me and Alex," he said, handing Tammy a bunch of flower weeds.

"Why thank you, Mr. Lucas," said Tammy, cupping his face. "My goodness, he's a miniature Joe. We better watch out for this one."

Tammy boiled the kettle. Buck and the cookie jar joined. We sipped tea and talked awkwardly for a minute.

"This tea, Tammy, I couldn't find it anywhere in Alderhill."

"It's so good, right? We get it in the Irish goods store. They ship over all sorts of stuff over. Their potato chips are something else." I was surprised Kate hadn't come to say hi.

"Is Kate out?"

"She was waiting so hard for you to get here, she finally lay down in her room and put her headphones in," said Tammy.

"Come on, Lucas. I need to introduce you to someone."

Even though the kitchen opened into the living room, Bailey had not come to say hello. She sat on the couch, watching TV. Her sea-green eyes glanced up at me as we passed through to my old bedroom—Kate's bedroom. She had straightened her reddish hair, which normally had a natural curl.

"Ok, Lucas. Go fetch the girl." I opened the door and sent him in while I listened outside.

"Oh, what's your name?" asked Kate in a baby voice.

"My sister told me you have a cat that's all white and has a dumb name but is really actually a cool cat."

Kate giggled. "You mean Buttons? She's not around."

"You mean she's dead? That's what Dad told me one time when I couldn't see our horse anywhere. So I told Dad, I'm going hunting for Star. I'll be back before dark. But Dad made this face and said no, Lucas, there's no point, because I don't think he's coming back."

Kate hissed laughter through her teeth like I knew she would. Lucas continued.

"Dad said he's gone to heaven because he was old and tired. We have another horse now. His name is Roly."

"Oh my, you're great at telling stories, aren't you?"

I cringed.

"So the cat is dead?" Lucas asked for confirmation.

"No, he's out somewhere, probably chasing mice."

Lucas must have spotted Kate's dancing posters.

"Hey, you can do that Irish? I can do it too. This is what Alex showed me."

Then I heard the blundering footsteps. I nudged the door open a crack. Kate's face was pure pleasure. She hobbled over to him with one crutch and swallowed him into her arms. "Oh my gosh, you are just the cutest." Then she spotted me. She shrieked almighty. "Oh my gosh. Oh. MY. Gosh! Alex! Can I keep him?"

Poor Lucas didn't know what was happening. She let go and hopped over crutches lying on the floor and hugged me 'round the waist until I couldn't breathe.

"I missed you, Kate."

"I missed you, Alexandi."

Lucas started jumping on the bed, and Kate went back to him. I looked 'round the room, walls still covered in posters of kittens and famous Irish dancers.

"He's the cutest thing ever."

Lucas came toward me, and I tried to hug him, but he ran straight by.

"There's the cat," he said, scampering out of the room.

Kate sat frowning.

"What's the matter?"

"Why did you leave?" she groaned.

"I had to. I really wish I didn't."

"Why did you, then?"

"Well, my mom and dad aren't quite as good as yours, and I had to go back and look after Lucas."

She pouted. "Why don't you and Lucas come live here with us?"

I sighed. "It doesn't work like that, I'm afraid." Kate pouted, which started to stress me out. "Come on, I need to make sure Lucas is behaving."

The sound of the TV in the living room had been replaced by the sound of quiet voices. I couldn't believe my eyes. Bailey was on the big couch, Lucas practically on her knee, the cat on his lap, and she was reading him a storybook.

"Hey," I said.

"Hey," she replied.

"Alex. I found the cat, and I found this here girl. Her names Bay Leaf and she's good at reading."

Bailey shrugged warmly. "Alex, fetch me some H2O, will you please?"

I smiled.

***

Lucas fell asleep on the couch, and we left him there as we ate Tammy's marinated chicken thighs, mashed potato and green beans. It was so warm and sticky, and the fan above swirled overtime trying to cool us all down. I took everything in — the fireplace, the collection of gaudy dance trophies on the shelf and the smell that was so synonymous with the Buckmans — a homey cinnamon smell.

"What's going on with the upstairs, Buck? That stair door has been locked ever since I first came here." The house was a duplex, but I had never been upstairs.

Buck grumbled. "We just get use of the downstairs." His eyes darted towards Tammy's then back to his plate.

"You mean you don't own this place?"

Buck shook his head. "Just renting."

Tammy and Buck settled down to TV early after dinner, but I felt like a mess after all the travel. I needed some air even though it was disgustingly humid out.

There was no AC, just a fan in every room, which didn't do much.

I passed through the living room on my way out and saw Kate's giant State Championship trophy on a shelf. Her name was engraved on the gold piece, and it filled me with magical energy as I read it with a mixture of pride and sadness.

Outside I sat on the porch swing, hoping for the tiniest of breezes. The clinking of mechanical sticks became louder as Kate joined, laying her crutches by her feet.

"Tell me everything about your dancing," she said.

"I found lessons on YouTube and learned all the beginner dances. I think I'm ready for harder steps now."

"Do you want to go to Kal McGettigan's workshop on Saturday?"

"I mean, I'd like to, but like, only if it's possible."

"I heard Mom say she would take you if you wanted."

"Amaze!" I said, smiling.

Kate pouted. We sat in silence, Kate dangling her one good leg over the side of the swing. Three months earlier, we had sat in the exact same spot in the freezing cold and dark, waiting for our ride to Cincinnati.

"You remember that, Kate?"

"When the doctor came in his big car?"

"And we set off on the adventure of a lifetime. Do you wish we hadn't?" I nodded towards her foot.

"No way!" she screamed. "Winning was the best feeling ever, and I will never forget. Now I know I can be the best in the world."

"But your leg, Kate. Aren't you miserable?"

"Oh, it's not that bad. It's not like I'm missing much, because I was never going to Nans even if I was able to."

"Nans?"

"North American Nationals? They were in Orlando last week. That's where Disneyworld is. My bestest dream would be to win Nans and go to Disneyworld. But it's ok. My leg is going to get better. I'll be stronger than ever. I read so on the internet." She started talking like a child robot, regurgitating information. "For a brief period, the fracture site is stronger than the surrounding bone. They later reach equal strength, and the fracture site is no more or less likely to break again."

I pursed my lips, impressed.

"It's weird you came this week. You know why? Because tomorrow is the day I get my cast off!" She wrapped her knuckles on the plaster.

"It is? Cool!"

"We are going to the hospital at lunch time, and they're going to get this big saw, and you'll see my leg for the first time in months, and the skin will be all soft and milky white and yucky, 'cause I seen it on the YouTube videos. The doctor—his name is Youssef—he has a funny voice." She took a quick breath and started mimicking. "Well and good, little Kate, you can be back on your feet and in the gym in maybe six weeks. You'll be like a ballerina again in no time."

Then she mock-laughed. "The doctor didn't even know what Irish dancing was, and I had to explain him and he still didn't know, so I made Mom do an over two-three. Then he shoved candy in my mouth as I tried to explain to him about everything."

I could only imagine. Kate grimaced.

"You're so lucky if you do go. Kal McGettigan is like, the all-time greatest dancer. Lucy's going and hopes he picks her to be in his new show. That or else to be his wife, which is impossible," she said, rolling her eyes. "Everyone wants to get picked for his new show. Do you remember Maura Wooldridge? Nicole and Sandra told me that Kal wanted Maura to be in his new show: that is, if he is actually making a new show. Can you imagine? Except Maura is already understudy in *Passion of the Dance* and isn't allowed to move."

"Wait, Maura who?"

"Don't you remember? We met her at State Championships last time?"

"That blonde kid? But she's like only my age?"

"Nuh-uh. She's eighteen. After World's in Montreal, she got auditioned for *Passion*. Now she's gonna be a superstar. They made her leave college, but it doesn't matter because she makes so much money, and she's even been in the magazines."

"You really think these workshops are auditions for his new show?"

Kate shrugged. "That's what people say. Although lots of different dance shows have summer workshops. *Passion* has one every summer in Dublin. They don't audition girls unless they've already danced in one of their summer schools. Then there's *Mystic River* and *Erin's Isle* and some others. Nicole says they are tons of fun."

We sat quietly for a minute, then I told Kate it was time for me to sleep. Before I left her, she was staring up at the sky, which was covered in a blanket of cloud. "Can you imagine what it would be like?" she said.

"What?"

"Doing what you love for life."

I left her to dream, slipped quietly into the bedroom and opened a window to let air circulate. Lucas was asleep on a cot at the end of the bed. My mind was buzzing. I thought about everyone I knew, Mom, Dad, Tammy, Buck. They all worked to pay the bills. Shouldn't everyone pay the bills doing work they loved rather than work they had to do? I thought how lucky Maura Woolridge was and gasped at how truly enormous the world of Irish dance seemed to be.

Chapter 12

I slept until 9:30 and woke as fresh as cream. Lucas was in the living room making the cat a house out of a large cardboard box.

"He's going to stay here until he has kittens. I saw him yesterday trying to crawl out an open window. We need the place in lockdown."

"H'ok," I said. I made myself a pot of coffee and sat out on the porch swing as the sun began to bake the planet. It shone yummy and warm on my forehead and beamed energy round my body.

I found a pair of Kate's yellow toy sunglasses in a wicker basket where keys were kept. They almost covered my entire face but didn't stop me from squinting. I sipped delicious coffee as a mower started up a couple houses over and briefly thought of Mom.

Then I jumped to my feet as something occurred to me. I went inside and grabbed an iPad and searched out Dr. Troy's secretary's number. It was a shot in the dark but worth a try. The previous year when I had attended Miller High, I had made some enemies, namely my cousin Bailey and her friends Vanessa and Dominique. After getting in a huge altercation and almost getting expelled from school, Vanessa's dad—Dr. Troy—a big-time doctor at the Cleveland Clinic, surprisingly exonerated me. He had done so much for me and was a major part of getting Kate and me to Cincinnati and getting us home after Kate's accident.

His secretary answered and said he was busy all day. Then I remembered he had given me his pager number on a business card one time. I found it being used as a bookmark in one of the books I had read that winter on Kate's bookshelf. I dialed the number. Just as I was about to hang up, he answered.

"Hello, Dr. Wallace? It's Alex Maslow."

"Hello, Alexandra," his deep voice said.

"Um, sorry to bother. I'm back in town. I'm actually going to the hospital with Kate later. I was just wondering if I could buy you a coffee, just to say thanks, ya know?"

He was quiet for a minute. "I guess I'll be in or around the cafeteria area at 12.30."

"Great. See you then," I said, excited.

Later that morning, a black guy called Winston drove by the house and picked up Buck. He had a baby face, a neat goatee and spiky locks of tight afro. Bailey came out to wave her dad off to work, but I knew the real reason behind that.

Winston was Buck's boss. He was starting his own business as a mechanic. Buck left smiling, so I guessed he was enjoying it.

Kate's hospital appointment wasn't until eleven. After breakfast I brought Lucas to Lakewood Park on Kate and Bailey's bikes. We stopped for ice cream on the way, the humidity of the night before gone and crystal blue sky leading the way. We cycled to Edgewater and stood at the cliff fence overlooking the lake and listened to the swishing of the water. There were a bunch of workers and machines and trucks a little farther along so we couldn't get right down to the rocks by the water, but from where we stood, we had a great view of downtown Cleveland, a city on the lake. It was a cool picture.

Lucas couldn't get over the vastness of the lake. I told him it froze during winter. He wanted to skate on it.

"Gosh, Alex, this city is really great!" he said.

I texted Vinnie to let him know we had arrived safe, but he just sent back a smiley face.

Then it was time to go to the hospital. The Cleveland Clinic was bigger than most towns I had visited in Kentucky. It had stores and restaurants and book shops and miles and miles of corridors. Lucas and Kate swapped roles as we hobbled down the halls to the reception.

"How did you break your leg?" Lucas asked.

"I had an accident."

"I bet you wish you drank more milk. Alex says that's why I gotta drink milk. My bones will never be brittle."

Tammy sniggered. When the receptionist realized how far we'd have to walk to the doctor's office, she organized a wheelchair for Kate. Of course, Lucas really wanted to ride in it.

They told Kate it would take almost an hour for the doctor to see her. I waited with them but soon got anxious as it neared time to meet with Dr. Troy. Lucas and I excused ourselves and headed for the cafeteria.

There he was, the familiar-looking big ol' graying beard of Dr. Troy, reading a newspaper, eating carrot cake and sipping tea.

"Coffee not good enough for ya, doctor?"

He didn't lower the newspaper.

"Gives me palpitations."

He shuffled the newspaper and continued reading. I tongued my cheek, wondering what to say next, but he made the decision for me.

"Please, sit." he said, folding the paper and pointing to the chair opposite. "How are you? Back on vacation?"

I rolled my eyes and wobbled my head. "Small getaway. You could say even in paradise the weather gets stormy once in a while."

"That's true." He pointed to his ring finger, which was missing some gold.

"This must be Lucas?"

"Say hello to Dr. Troy," I said.

Lucas inched over onto my lap and didn't say a word.

"Things have turned real bad again, doctor. Mom can't stop drinking, and when that happens, it's all yelling. And you never know which way she's going to be."

The doctor nodded. "There must be some counselling services available? There are pills your mom could take that would take the edge off."

"Mom won't admit to anything being wrong. Dr. Troy, how can we get some actual help?"

"Sounds like your folks have long-term addiction problems, and unfortunately, unless they really want to be helped, you can't force them to change their ways."

"But what about us? It's not fair on us!" I said, getting animated, bobbing Lucas on my knee.

The doctor was solemn. "I've seen many families just like yours." He wiggled his finger and with a smile, poked Lucas, who was nuzzling into my neck. "Lucas. Do you like it in Cleveland?"

"Yes, mister."

"Are you looking forward to going back home?" He shook his head no. "Why not?"

"I just wanna stay with Alex."

"Won't you miss your mom and dad?"

A silence hung. I rocked him some more.

"There is a danger he could struggle in his formative years…unless there's some intervention, but I'm afraid Kentucky is out of my jurisdiction. Tell me, is she ever physical?"

My eyes wavered. "Not with us. Dad gets the brunt of it. But it's only a matter of time."

"How old are you?"

"Um, fifteen."

He grimaced. "Eighteen is the legal age for adoption in Kentucky…Not saying that's what you should do. I suggest you see your family doctor in Alderhill and have them start a line of enquiry."

"But those people are so slow. They don't do anything; they don't take anything seriously."

Dr. Troy was quiet a second. "Alex, I do have one idea. If things are as bad as you say…You might not like it, though."

***

Dr. Troy went back to work, and Lucas and I ran back to the waiting room, my mind whirling with what he had said. We got there just in time to see Kate's cast being sawn off. Lucas's eyes went all white, and he gripped my hand as the saw buzzed.

"They're gonna chop her leg off."

"No they aren't, silly. Just watch." I pulled him into me and allowed my arms rest around his shoulders as we stood to the side of the doctor's table.

Kate didn't wince or close her eyes once despite the terrifying scene and noise. She smiled, excited to see her poor leg again. Then they washed her yucky leg before the doctor checked it over.

The injured leg was so different to the other — skinny, white and fragile.

"Now miss, let's see how it feels." His eyebrows did the urging.

Kate hesitantly put her foot on the ground. She looked for affirmation from the doctor, then she took a few slow steps across the white hospital floor. When she turned, I saw her wince.

"How does it feel?"

She didn't answer, but a tear ran down her cheek.

"It's ok," she said. She took a few more steps back before pausing.

"Does it hurt?" the doctor asked.

Kate walked back to the bench. Finally, she said no.

"Kate. You have to tell the truth," said Tammy. "Does it hurt even a little?"

Kate nodded and started crying. "It hurts. A lot!"

The doctor frowned briefly. He looked at Tammy. "Let's get it x-rayed and see what exactly's going on."

Lucas played with the cast that had been split in two and lay on the white tile floor.

"Can I keep it, Alex?"

"Ew, Lucas, gross. No, you cannot keep it."

Kate hobbled after the doctor and went to get her leg x-rayed, which didn't take long. Soon they were back.

"The radiologist will have a proper look at the x-ray shortly," he said before pausing and looking into Kate's big, anxious eyes.

He glanced up at Tammy and exhaled. "Mrs. Buckman. I shouldn't really say without final word from the radiologist, but it looks like the bone has not healed as expected."

"What?" asked Tammy, covering her mouth.

"Kate shouldn't have any pain. It looks like the tibia has not healed evenly."

There was a silence in the room, and even Lucas stopped murmuring. The doctor held up the x-ray and with his pen, began pointing.

"Here you can see that the right leg is slightly shorter than the left."

There was an awful silence for a split second, broken by Lucas, who giggled. He started walking 'round the room in circles like a pirate with a peg leg.

"Look here, Alex." He sniggered and bobbed around, using his arms for balance. My eyes widened, and I clasped my hand to my mouth as I watched the color drain from Kate's face. Tammy smoothly slid across and put a gentle hand on his brow and hushed him like an expert kid whisperer.

"What does this mean, Mom?" asked Kate.

"Can you fix it?" asked Tammy.

"Like I said, I have to wait for the radiologist to confirm."

"Might I never be able to dance again?" Kate whimpered, her face the same pale shade as her gimpy leg. She stared at it in such disappointment, angry at her body for not healing correctly.

"I can't answer that."

"But it's likely she will?" Tammy urged him with her eyes, almost wanting him to lie if he had to.

"The chances are possibly 40-50%, I'm afraid. Hopefully she will be able to walk properly, maybe run a little."

My head started to spin. Tammy stood up fast.

"Can I speak to you outside a moment, doctor?"

I went to Kate. My heart was beating hard.

"I'm sure they can do another operation and everything will be fine," I said, trying to be strong, but my voice failing me.

"The doctor said it, Alex. I might not dance anymore." She said it so crystal clear, without a flinch. She must have been in shock. I realized I was holding my breath, and I couldn't swallow; it was as if a molten rock fresh from a volcano lay in the back of my throat. Lucas stared at me anxiously. Tears started to gather at the corner of my eyes.

"But Kate," I said, my breath catching. "But…Kate?"

"It's ok, Alex," she said quietly. "Sometimes bad things happen."

"You love dancing. You will dance again."

I full-on cried now and couldn't stop. Kate was quiet, her pretty little face and eyes determined.

"Alex," she said after a moment. "You know I wanted to be the best in the world? I wanted to win World Championships. But now I can't. Alex?"

"Yes?"

"Will you do me a favor?"

"Anything."

"I want you to win for me."

"Win? Win what?"

"World's."

My head swam. What was this kid asking? She was asking me to do something impossible, to live out her dreams. It was the most ridiculous request on earth, but I looked at her teary, starry eyes and couldn't say anything.

"Alex. Please win it for me?"

"That's crazy. I won't win it for you. Kate, I promise to help you get better. I will help you win. I'll help you. I swear it. We'll dance together."

And we hugged.

Chapter 13

The beginner's class was at ten the following day at the Westin Hotel downtown, but dancing was the last thing on my mind. I had a terrible night's sleep, as the longest train in the history of trains passed through Lakewood blowing its horn for twenty minutes solid, and no sooner had I fallen back into a deep sleep, some gentle piano playing in the living room woke me once more. I decided to get up.

"Morning, Kate," I said plonking down on the couch, rubbing the sleep from my eyes. She looked sad. "What's the matter?"

"Oh, just saying goodbye to the piano."

"Huh?"

"Some men are coming to take it away. Mom says we need the money."

It was so depressing. To make matters worse, Lucas had a permanent smile on his face, running around without a care in the world.

At nine-fifteen, Kate found me relaxing on the couch, watching cartoons with Lucas. She peeled a banana and shoved it into my mouth, steely-faced.

"Are we still doing this?" I asked.

"Get your dance things. Mom says we're leaving soon."

The free class was a sweetener for the moms who were spending huge money to send their older kids to the real thing.

There were hundreds of kids in the dance hall, aged between four and maybe twelve. There were only three kids my age. Everybody crowded around Kal McGettigan for selfies and autographs. Kate lost her mind squealing when she saw him, and I could kinda see why. He was Irish via Hawaii and California. Hell yeah! He wasn't overly tall but V-shaped, with a dark tan and full black hair. You could tell why he had been a principal dancer, because he oozed a certain something.

He took time out to talk specially to Kate when he saw her on crutches. He knew all about her injury from State Champs the spring before and told her to never give up on her dreams. My stare-down was interrupted when two older female dance teachers called us onto the floor to start the lesson. Tammy took Kate and Lucas to the aquarium for an hour. The teachers were probably in their late twenties, dressed in black yoga pants and white vests. They were so strong looking, every muscle completely toned.

After warm-ups we put on our soft shoes and did drills followed by a step down the line. At first, I couldn't concentrate, my eyes constantly darting to see where Kal was. He wasn't paying attention, mainly talking to parents and organizers. Then our teachers separated us into groups that I guessed were based on ability. A third teacher came in to help because of the huge numbers. I was placed in a smaller group with about twenty others.

My teacher was called Diane. She had a sing-song Irish accent and long brown hair almost to her butt. She taught us the primary reel, which I found easy after all those hours I'd spent practicing in my barn. But Diane had so many corrections for me and would not leave me alone, almost to the point where I thought she hated me. One of the parts was a skip two change, and you had to swing your leg up, and I really loved that. I could swing my leg high above my head and kept doing it, trying to show off.

Finally, Kal McGettigan made his appearance, walking around, gently touching the dancers where their backs were arched, pushing a shoulder back. I pushed my chest out hoping he would notice. He walked towards me, and I felt as if my legs were dancing like live chopsticks. He stood to my side and after a second, yanked my shoulders back. I stopped dancing, and his eyes pierced mine. He made a royal motion with his hand.

"Lift your chin a little." I did so. "You're arching your back too much. Why? You weren't doing it a couple of minutes ago?"

I blushed. He was quite stern, and I wasn't sure if he was being mean or if it was his way.

"How long have you been dancing?"

"Um, like a month or two?"

"And do you have a teacher?"

I shook my head and mumbled no. Was it that obvious?

"I thought so. I saw Diane working with you. Your steps have been smooth ever since."

He seemed quite a deep person at that point, frowning in contemplation, probably a million things on his mind, but surprisingly, a smile emerged and he nodded to himself. He dropped his head to the side half an inch and squinted.

"Did you dance ballet?" I nodded. "Your movements are graceful, but you're landing like a ballet dancer instead of like an Irish dancer. You need to land on your toes. Like this."

He took a step backwards and demonstrated. And when he leaped and landed so close to me, it was like the difference between standing next to a Ferrari versus a Ford. He smiled and moved on to the next girl.

I continued dancing and worked on what he said about landing, and the more I concentrated, the more I felt my face redden and sweat build on my forehead. I caught a glimpse of Kal looking at me another time and felt so embarrassed; how ugly I must have looked.

The class ended with some stretching. I felt a tap on my shoulder as I tied my sneakers.

"You pick things up quickly. What's your name?

"Um, Alex." I sniffled.

Again his face was serious. I knew he had just complimented me, but it felt like I had been scolded. Then came a surprise.

"I really like the way you dance. It's got lots of charm. And your eyes have fire. You should probably find yourself a dance class and start competing, maybe see if you could progress a little more."

I had not been expecting that and blushed hard. Kal pondered, and all the while, his fingers danced Irish steps on the palm of his hand. "Are you attending the rest of my workshop?"

I cleared my throat. "I can't. I'm just visiting for the weekend."

"Cute accent. Virginia?"

"No, Kentucky."

"Interesting. Here's an idea. Sorry, I'm just curious now," he said, genuinely apologetic. "If you like, you can stay for the next hour. I'm keen to see how you fare with some harder material. After all, you've come a long way..."

I swallowed hard. "Um, I guess I just need to ask my aunt if that's ok?"

He looked at me, and I waited for him to say something and quickly realized he wanted me to run along and get permission. I quick walked outside and found Tammy was waiting with some other moms. Kate and Lucas were playing with another girl. The words came rattling out of my mouth.

"Tam, Tammy, Kal—Mr. McGettigan asked me to stay for an extra hour, is that ok? Huh?" I gasped for breath. Tammy frowned in confusion. I started back into it. "The man said nice things, and he was like, stay for another hour and learn more, and so is that ok, Tam, for you to wait for me like one more hour? Please, of course?"

"I guess so," she said, her eyes floating and looking from me to her friend, to Kate and then back to me.

"Thanks," I said, and ran back. It was the most excited I had felt in years.

Chapter 14

Around thirty kids aged between twelve and eighteen entered the studio, all with serious faces and serious gear. I had no competition trying to hide at the back of the dance floor, with most girls competing for front floor space and Kal's attention.

After warm up and stretches, we went straight into drills. Kal put me in the last group of five so that I could get a moment to learn which way to go and what not. First we worked on our swing. Then they did this move called a bird. I tried to imitate it as best I could along with my group as we worked our way from the back of the hall to the front, then fizzled back around the sides to do it again.

The bird was basically an over without changing legs. I felt so dumb the first few times 'cause I was messing it up, but I concentrated hard watching the other dancers and slowly got my head around it.

After drills we were again split up based on ability. Everyone bar me were Open Competition dancers, but Kal worked with dancers that were World qualifiers. Again Diane was my teacher. It was soft shoe dancing for the early part of the afternoon. Diane added a turn to my primary reel and basically took turns watching the dancers and correcting things. She spent a long time helping me get the turn right and getting me to cross over and stay on my toes. After twenty minutes hard work, I was really getting into the rhythm of the workshop and felt my confidence growing.

As we broke for a drink at the end of the hour, I slipped into my sneakers, ready to go, when Kal came over to me.

"Well done, Alex. You have a real hunger to improve."

"Thanks, Mr. McGettigan," I said, too exhausted for shyness.

He handed me a leaflet. It was for a week-long summer school the third week of August. The price for the week was six hundred dollars.

"I hope you keep it up. If you can come back for my week-long workshop later this summer, we could make some serious progress."

"Um, no offense, mister, but this costs a little too much for me."

He nodded and did this mouth shrug. "Well, there is a *Dance Teachers Commemorative Union.* They offer scholarships and small bursaries to certain dancers...I could write you a little letter that might help get you some money to help pay..." Then he paused and smiled kindly. "Just an idea. My work email is at the bottom."

"Ok, thanks," I said, a little dazed.

"Keep practicing, whatever you do. You're lucky to have real natural talent. Don't let it go to waste." He spun 'round and walked off. I almost died as my heart swam around my chest.

When I told Kate, her eyes sparkled. She tensed her arms in the air, and they vibrated like a baby bird on the verge of flight.

"Oh my gosh! See, I wasn't being dumb asking you to win World's for me. I wonder if he wants you to be in his new show! We need to dance so much right now."

Her mouth was running overdrive, and I was still shaking. Tammy put her arm round my back and gave me a half hug.

"Nice Job, Alex. But take some of what he said with a pinch of salt."

"What you mean, Tam?"

"Yeah, what do you mean, Mom?"

"Oh, these big shots. They can be such schmoozers."

"I don't know what that is, but you are wrong, Mom." said Kate. "Alex, you need to save and come back at the end of August. Ok?"

I did not know where my mind had gone. Kate poked me with her crutch as we moved along.

"Oh poop. Look, it's Jessica Harvey."

"Hmm, what?" I said, still in my own bubble before noticing one of the dancers returning from the bathroom. I had noticed her earlier, front and center, always trying to catch Kal's attention. She had a small pretty face and was petite of stature but maturely developed. I accidently locked eyes with her, and she returned the stare. Her eyes were dark orange, like the embers of a fire. She gave me the creeps.

"What's her deal?"

"It's not going to be as straightforward as we thought. I didn't realize she would come all the way from Chicago."

"What do you mean?" I asked.

"Jessica is three-time World Champion. She's amazing. I follow her on Insta. She has like fifty thousand followers. Hey Mom, why didn't Jessica go to a masterclass in Chicago?"

Tammy cleared her throat, wanting to whisper. "These workshops are only being held in Cleveland, New York and Los Angeles."

"O.M.G! She's come all this way to show off to Kal." said Kate.

"Big whoop," I said, feeling utmost confidence.

"But Alex," said Kate as we went through the revolving door. "She's the same age as you."

Kate exited, but I continued in the revolving door for a couple more cycles. When I got out, Kate was kneeling on the ground, laughing. I walked onwards, mimicking a zombie.

"So scared. Jessica gonna eat me."

We got in the car and made tracks back to Lakewood. Something struck me, and I turned to Tammy.

"Why did Kal choose Cleveland for a masterclass?"

Tammy grunted. "Beats me."

But Kate started giggling like crazy in the back. "You know how boys usually have a girlfriend? Well, Kal is married. To another boy!"

"How modern." I smiled.

"His husband is from Cleveland," said Tammy with a frank expression.

***

On Sunday evening, we went to this restaurant I liked called O'Malley's. Every time Kate went to take a bite of food, she'd start talking. Everyone had almost finished eating, and she was still talking. I tried to pay for the food, but neither Buck nor Tammy would hear of it.

"You need all your money for August. Kal will be expecting you. He can help you get so much better, and now that he knows you, you need to make sure he doesn't forget you, especially with Jessica Harvey right there in his face the whole time."

I was torn between the excitement at Kal's words and depression at the fact that Kate actually wanted me to try and win World's for her. That and the whole going home to Alderhill business. But it made Kate happy to talk about it.

I caught Tammy looking at me with sad eyes every now and then, and that reminded me. The last time we had been to O'Malley's, Tammy had acted real weird and actually started crying.

Kate was not done talking.

"You are on his radar now. I read on Facebook the girl who won *Reel Rebels* is going to Kal's New York workshops. You know what that means? It means he's getting dancers he likes all together for his new show!"

Kate took the briefest of breaths. "When you start dancing, you can make lots of money and bring Lucas with you everywhere so he doesn't need to stay with your wicked mom and dad."

Tammy butted in. "Kate, go easy. Maybe Alex doesn't want to get all serious and just wants to have some fun dancing."

"It's too late. She's already agreed to try and win World's for me," said Kate.

"Is that so?" said Tammy, and she looked like she had more to say, but Buck gave her a look and a 'fuhgeddaboudit' hand gesture, and she stopped.

But I didn't mind Kate's babbling, because maybe what she was saying made sense. The dance expert said I was good and that I should keep practicing. It wasn't impossible to improve quickly. The idea of one day dancing in a show seemed amazing and not unrealistic. I was glowing inside.

Soon after it was time for Buck to bring us to the bus station. We all hugged goodbye. Lucas had made cards for everyone. Tammy eyed me different, as if it was finally hitting home the ugly life Lucas and I were returning to.

"Take care of yourself and your brother. We're all hoping for you here," she said.

Kate came with us and sat in the back with Lucas, the quietest she had been all weekend. She held Lucas's hand the whole time.

"We wish things were different. Life's a little too conventional when you're not around," said Buck as we all hugged goodbye.

I couldn't sleep on the bus ride back to Kentucky. My mind whirled over and over with the same thoughts — dance, Kate, hopes that Mom would make a miraculous transformation. The uncertainty surrounding our immediate life made me nauseous.

Chapter 15

Grandpa collected us from the bus station after one AM, and we stayed with him that night. Dad picked us up the following morning. He was wearing his army uniform and would go straight to Fort Knox army base after.

"Don't you guys fret, everything's just fine. Your mom's got some medicines to help her rest. She needs lots and lots of sleep," said Dad.

But I didn't trust medicine.

Mom sat like a zombie, watching TV. She smiled hello, as if oblivious to what had gone on before. She talked quietly to herself, saying that she might like to take Roly for a ride. I went to make us something to eat, but there was nothing except cereal. There was no milk. Part of me wanted to yell like crazy at Mom, and another part felt so bad for her. The best idea my tired brain could think of was to go to Vinnie's for breakfast and while there, make a sandwich to bring back to Lucas.

I was so excited to tell him what Kal had said.

His mom's car was gone so I let myself in quietly, hoping to surprise him. He wasn't plonked in front of the sofa, and the Xbox hadn't been turned on, so I figured he was still in bed. Even though it was almost midday, he needed all the sleep he could get, being a growing boy and all. Sleep helped muscles grow, or so he'd told me when I'd tried to get my two hands round his biceps. He was in for a nice surprise.

I turned the handle slowly. A dark-haired girl leapt from the bed, whites of her eyes lighting up the room. Vinnie shot upright. My heart fluttered and floated into the air like a helium balloon before exploding.

"What the hell?" I yelled.

"Alex?"

The girl was Kimberly, a ninth grader from school. She looked at me with her frightened eyes, collected her things and scampered out the door.

Vinnie laughed nervously. "It's not what you think, Alex,"

"Not what I think? You're giving me b.s television lines?"

"We were just kissing, that's all. Didn't mean nothing."

He pulled on a t-shirt from the side of the bed. I couldn't conjure a reply. I stared hard. Even though he was the same Vinnie I had fallen in love with the previous winter, he looked a little fresh, a little wild. I was aching inside. All the times I had thought of him when I'd been taken to Cleveland that previous winter, longing for his presence and love. And the feelings of joy I'd felt when I came back, that first kiss and how my body ached with love. I refused to let myself cry.

"Do you love her?" I whispered.

He let out a mighty sigh. "Jeez, Alex, 'course I don't."

My mouth was pursed. He exhaled a little more evenly and walked toward me, his arms opening to swallow me up. I had a mixture of anger and hurt and love and everything. I wanted to hurt him. I wanted to lash out at his face with my nails, but when I sunk into his beating chest and his manly smell enveloped me, I melted. He looked down at me with his penetrating brown eyes and kissed me with his big fat bottom lip. But a fire had been lit. I pushed him away with all my might.

"NO!"

I knocked over a plant pot as I ran outside. Vinnie called my name, but the sounds became removed and floated into the sky without meaning. The sun beat down onto the green grass, the colors seeming so illuminated, but the world at that moment felt so strange I could hardly make anything out. It was as if I had died, and my spirit was rising into space, and all the colors and objects and smells were melting into one.

Vinnie's mom's car pulled up. She said my name and looked at me strange. I was holding my little red bike. And it happened suddenly. I just got sick. I puked everywhere, real violent, getting some on my hand and my jeans and my Converse. Vinnie's mom held me round the waist with concern. I wiped my mouth on my sleeve and looked at her blankly. Vinnie called to me from the front door, but I picked up my bike, swung my leg over and started peddling, sucking air, trying to cool the flames in my throat.

I was shaking all over when I finally got up the hill to my house. I dropped the bike at the front door and with my last ounce of energy, dragged myself to the kitchen and shoved my face under the faucet, trying to extinguish the fire in my chest. Lucas was staring at me, an army figure in his hand. I went in the bedroom and closed my eyes. I was still shivering. I lay there until my organs started regulating whatever the heck was going on.

I thought to myself and didn't find it funny. The more things changed, the more things stayed the same.

You couldn't depend on anyone else for your happiness. I cried, knowing it was over for me and Vinnie, knowing there was no way back for my first love. I called Michelle and told her.

"Alex, girl. You know I love Vinnie too, but trust me, if a boy did that to me that would be the end."

Perhaps Mom and Dad could have done with a friend like Michelle right before they decided to go making mistakes.

"What a dumb shithead," she said. "There ain't nothing for it. You know what you gotta do?"

"What?"

And she told me. Soon as I hung up, I stripped off my camouflage t-shirt and torn jeans and check shirt and put on some old sweat pants and a black shirt, which was the only clean thing I could find. I gathered up all the clothes Vinnie had given me and anything that reminded me of him, and I carried them to the barn with some matches and a firelighter and found an old steel drum.

Mom, combing Roly, watched me as I lit the fire and dropped the items in one by one and wept quietly. I waited until the smoke was no more and everything had turned to ash. All the while, Mom brushed Roly. Finally, as she passed, she put her arm 'round my shoulder and whispered in a sleepy voice.

"Sorry, Alex. That's all mens are, but cheatin' s.o.b's."

***

Afterwards I walked down the fields to my rock and sat and thought and listened to the birds singing and to the sound of Lucas bouncing the ball against our trailer. The sun was glorious, and I took my sweatshirt off and let the hot breeze smack me in the face. I wondered what it was like for other kids who got everything they needed and asked for—not video games and dolls and clothes and phones but things like food and warmth and love and affection.

I was supplying a whole family-full of affection to keep Lucas alive. And no one was caring for me. I thought of Kate. I had so much anger, and it simmered just right. I wiped those few tears and promised they would be my last.

My mind became clear. Nothing good ever happened, and you had to work especially hard to make things just ok. I was going to take control of my destiny. I thought about the spectrum of good and bad. Here I was at the brown end of the spectrum, and Jessica Harvey at the gold end. I had thought that somewhere in the middle would do, but now the middle wouldn't be the goal any more. I wanted the good life, for me, for Lucas.

Kate had said something that stuck in my mind one time. She said it was LeBron, but it was actually Jordan. He said, "Do you want it or just kinda want it?" I was done just 'kinda' wanting it. Life threw crap at you, and it would continue to do so if you let it. I wasn't going to let it anymore.

I had made a promise to Kate, one that seemed to defy the laws of reality. But maybe, just maybe, I could achieve. Kate always said dream big. I believed my family would forever go to hell and back and never even get a tan, that things were always meant to be this way, and by believing this prophecy, so it was. We were all born superstars; it was our minds that held us back or propelled us toward happiness.

I thought about what Dr. Troy had said, if things didn't work out for Mom with her medicines, and hoped it wouldn't come to that. Once I changed one area of my life, the rest would fall into place like a chorus line of dancers. I thought about what Kal McGettigan had said and started believing it was possible to become a successful dancer. It was time to take care of me, and I had a mission. And that started with finding a dance teacher. It was time for Lucas and me to go visit Grandpa.

The cycle focused my mind and emotions. Lucas spoke to himself in relaxed tones the whole way. I daydreamed that life was great. The blinding sunlight and the vanilla scent of summer and the passing trucks and crickets croaking helped my mind wander. I imagined that the warm rays of blinding sun were guiding me as I peddled with eyes closed briefly and that I was enveloped by a glow of love. Without the stress of Mom and Dad, my life would be a joy. And that was funny, because other people, they strived different, it was just all depending. Some strived for success, law firms, business, health, politics. Here we were striving for survival as success. That was messed up.

It was almost as if the universe was listening to me, 'cause we passed a billboard advertising *Passion of the Dance* coming to Lexington. Soon as I went on Grandpa's computer, dance stuff appeared. On my Facebook page, adverts popped up about Irish dance classes or shows or Ireland and whatnot. It was like those guys at Google and Facebook were teaming up to subliminally drive me Irish dance crazy with their algorithms. Grandpa made ice tea and took Lucas out to the yard.

I started off searching anything I could find to do with Kal McGettigan. I found a link to the *Reel Rebels* series, which seemed pretty cool. Then I watched YouTube clips of *Passion of the Dance*. Kal's dancing was mesmerizing, and his feet were out of control. I tingled as I watched the encore and cast smiling. The stage magic and chemistry looked wonderful.

Then I searched Alderhill and the whole of Kentucky for an Irish dance class, but the closest was twenty-five miles away in Windsor.

I wished someone like Kate or even her friend Martin, who was an insanely good dancer for a nine-year-old, lived nearby. I laughed as I remembered the freckled, juiced-up goon. Then by total coincidence, I came across a Parade of Champions. Martin's older brother Declan appeared having won All Ireland's. I'd briefly met him at State Championships in Cincinnati. He was real Irish, kinda sweet and an amazing dancer—just the kind of person I needed.

Then I remembered a St. Paddy's Day parade in Alderhill a couple of years back. One of the floats had a couple playing an accordion and a violin and some round, one-handed drum and they had four old gals and two guys doing formation Irish steps. I remembered because at the time it struck me as weird—some of the dancers were Grandpa-old. Someone had recorded the parade and posted it on YouTube. They danced as the float drove along slowly, and it was impressive—despite the steps being simple, the crisscrossing formation was intricate and well-rehearsed. I read the credits and found the name Mr. F. Anderson. With a little more searching, I found that he worked in the county arts department at the town hall in Alderhill. He was the guy I had to talk to.

I went outside and yelled to Grandpa. Lucas was digging a hole in the dirt.

"Grandpa, can I take your car?"

He wiped his brow and put the shovel down. "I need a rest. Where we headed?"

"Just to the town hall."

He jammed the shovel into the dirt and looked at it as if to tell it to 'stay', and soon we were in his wagon, windows rolled down, hot as the sun inside.

Chapter 16

Grandpa parked the car across from the old town hall, and he and Lucas went to get ice cream. Lucas was burning up like a flare.

The town hall was all colonial and smart on the outside, red-bricked with pillars and an arch doorway with statues and what not, and inside was like Congress or something, or like where the queen might have come to stay in an Airbnb back in the day. Reception told me that Fuzz Anderson was the director.

"Seriously?"

"Why, ma'am, what seems to be the problem?"

"I need to speak to Fuzz?" I said those words and questioned my sanity.

"Have you got a meeting, darlin'?"

"Yes," I lied. I spied the clock, which said quarter to two.

"It's for two PM. Sorry, I'm a little early. I like to be…early…"

"Have a seat, ma'am," she said, pointing behind me to where there was a bench at the back wall underneath old paintings of important people. I sat for a second and could see down the corridor where she had glanced and figured that was where his office was. The door was open a little.

Once the receptionist became sufficiently distracted, I made a run for it and knocked gently on the door.

"Come in," a voice sang. I closed the door behind me. The guy was tugging on a venetian blind that was stuck one side up, one side half-way there. He wore light gray suit pants with a matching vest and a dark blue shirt. He turned, and my mouth dropped. He was wearing a pink bow-tie, small round spectacles and a very, very neat moustache. His black boots had a strap and a silver buckle.

Well, well, I thought. Not what I had expected.

"Mister Anderson? My name is Alex, and I don't have an appointment, but I only want one minute of your time."

His next words surprised me. His voice was no longer lyrical. It was deep — not quite old Buck deep, but trombone-esque all the same. It sounded like it had just broken and had the potential to go from base to tenor without warning.

"Aren't you a fiery one. Do you act?"

"No. Mr. Anderson, I was wondering —"

"We started a drama society, and we're always looking for new people, especially lil' hotties like yourself. How old are you? Nineteen? Twenty?"

"Fifteen."

He raised his eyebrows.

"Anyway, Fuzz. Here's my question. A few years ago, the town had a St. Paddy's Day parade?"

"You're Irish? I'd never have guessed. Where are your freckles?"

He giggled to himself. My mouth hung open a second, but I persevered.

"There were some older people Irish dancing on the back of a truck?"

"You know, my grandma—she was Jewish. She thought she was Irish, though, because she had this real light reddish hair on her arm and some freckles here and there. My grandpa said she must have sat on an Irish person once and that's how she got freckles on her butt!"

I clicked my fingers. "Fuzz? Fuzz? I'll be out of your hair in one minute. How do you do with direct questions?"

"Well, sure, if you get to the point?"

"This is a matter of life and death."

"Oh, kind of like Apollo 13?" he asked, hopeful.

"No more, like Apollo 1."

"I'm not familiar with that mission…"

"It blew up, killing the three astronauts on board…" I said frankly.

He rubbed his hands, and his eyes sparkled. "Oh, this is urgent. Go on…"

"Well, my little cousin Kate, in Cleveland…We ran away together to State Champs in Cincinnati last March because it was her dream, and she won, but she ended up breaking her leg—"

"Is she gonna be ok?"

"That's the thing, Fuzz. It's serious. She got me into dancing, so I wanna be able to do that with her when she's better."

"That's it?"

"Well, no, not exactly."

"Please continue…"

I paused, feeling dumb. "Mr. Anderson. Fuzz. Kate thinks I'm good, that I've got Irish dance smarts, and everything she's showed me is super easy. And at the free dance class with Kal McGettigan—he said I should come back for the masterclass. So he must think I'm good too." I paused. "I need to become a champion and get into one of those shows. I think it may save my life." I paused as he grinned in disbelief, one finger tapping his chin. "Also, and this part is crucial: I may need this to help me with a very fragile family situation."

"And what exactly can I do?"

"Can you introduce me to the guy who trained those old folks for the parade so I can get started? I gotta get started now. I'm already fifteen and too old. I know it's not going to be easy, but I figure it's worth a shot, right?"

I exaggerated a smile his way. His face was intense. He stretched his hand towards me, and I stared at it. He nodded earnestly, but I kept staring.

"I'm your guy."

My mouth dropped open. Still smiling, he withdrew his hand and picked up his cell phone from the desk.

"This is so exciting. Wait 'til I tell my wife!"

***

Fuzzy didn't have one Irish bone in his body but had fallen in love with Irish dancing after seeing a commercial on TV when he was a kid. He'd started taking classes aged eleven. His mom had passed away when he was a baby, so his dad had driven him all around Maryland to competitions. Fuzzy'd placed top ten at North American Nationals back in the day, which didn't sound all that impressive, seeing as there couldn't have been many men dancing back in the day.

"You danced in a show?"

"Yes indeedy. Why are you surprised?"

"Oh, it's just I thought you had to be top ten in the World to dance in shows?"

He laughed. "I may not have been a champion, but you need other qualities that can make up for average ability."

"Like what?"

"Charisma and stage presence!" He winked at me to prove his point. He was an attractive man, but that stunk like cheese.

"I was in a show much smaller than *Passion,* but it was still good. It was called *Mystic River.* We toured a lot. Mainly China, though."

"China?" I yelped.

"Yup, they go crazy for Irish dancing over there."

For some reason, Fuzz liked my story. He was happy to teach me on the condition that I would help out with next year's St. Patrick's Day parade. He said that they always needed people for charity dinner entertainment and the likes and that I could come in useful. I bounced out of that town hall like I was riding a space hopper.

"My lord, is that what your teeth look like when you don't grimace?" said Grandpa as I got in the car.

"Good news, Grandpa. I found myself an Irish dance tutor."

"Oh," he said, disappointed. "Thought maybe we had won the lottery."

The next day, I practiced for forty minutes, which was the longest yet. I knew I'd have to work hard at a proper class with Fuzz. I could dance the steps real nice for the first twenty minutes, but as soon as I pushed through, no matter how hard I tried, I stopped kicking my butt and crossing my feet in the sidestep. My legs turned to jelly.

The following day, I rested. Dad went to work early and said he was going to the army base afterward. There seemed to be trouble brewing somewhere in the Middle East, and they were fetching idiots from all sorts of places to get killed in the name of America. Mom was still dumb from meds.

My body and brain felt exhausted. I found Lucas playing outside in the rain. I gave him a shower, made some hot chocolate and settled us both down in the bedroom with an old TV and VCR I'd found in the barn. We watched Mom and Dad's wedding video curled up in bed as lighting struck and thunder roared.

Everyone looked so dated with their old-style clothing and weird hair-cuts. All the same, Dad looked so handsome—tall, lean, broad shoulders, and I couldn't get over Mom. She wasn't just pretty, she was superstar pretty. Her face wasn't so narrow, and she had the most beautiful smile. They looked so happy together walking up the aisle and at their first dance, cheeks touching. But I guess everyone looked happy on their wedding day. Wasn't it a requirement? I hoped we were on the road back to that kind of happiness.

I spotted myself, the flower girl. I couldn't have been more than Lucas's age, maybe five. I was chasing and fighting with a boy, like a gritty angel trying to get my toy back and his interest.

"That kid looks like me," said Lucas. "Did I have long hair when I was younger?"

"That's me, dummy," I yelled. "What you mean when you were younger? You weren't even a sperm then."

"What's a sperm?"

Whoops, I thought. "You weren't going to be born for another…" I counted quick on my fingers, too tired for mental arithmetic. "For another ten years or so."

I pointed out Grandpa and Grandma, some neighbors. It had been a small affair in a barn decorated all nice with hanging baskets and candles and bouquets of flowers and old wooden benches.

We fast-forwarded, and Lucas enjoyed watching everything go fast, people moving 'round all fast. He started moving his head 'round fast, trying to talk fast, walking to the door fast, just like them.

"Hey, sit down, would ya," I yelped when his exuberance got the better of him and he stood on my foot.

He was hurt a minute, and I felt terrible. We snuggled again and watched the end of the tape, the storm outside getting wilder. Mom was getting drunk at her own wedding. She was all smiles and dancing but mainly stumbling. The tape ended, and Lucas was asleep up against me, and I lay there listening, sad as the thunder crackled and the blue flickers of lightning lit our cozy bedroom.

Chapter 17

I was so excited for my first dance class with Fuzzy that Saturday. I practiced so hard in the days leading up as I tried to escape the constant pinging of my phone as alerts to Vinnie's regret flooded in.

Dad was resting on the porch, hands on his knees. My shoulders dropped when I saw the can of beer.

"Jesus, Dad!"

He looked at me, kind. "What, honey? Come on, it's the weekend!"

"Every day's the weekend," I said and sat on the wooden boards beside him. He scratched the top of my head with his fingernails. I loved it when he did that.

"How many those you had?"

"Just a sip."

"Can you drive after a sip?" He nodded. "C'mon. Get your keys."

It was a twenty-minute ride to Anderson's Yard. The guy worked for the government, and it showed. He had a gorgeous home made with red bricks and four high chimneys, two on either gable. It was in a lush field surrounded by more fields and trees. A stream rolled down the bottom of the yard, heading lord knows where. They had a barn twice the size of their house. I climbed some steep wooden steps, knocked on the front door and let myself in. Inside was all opened up, the hallway with the stairs in the middle looking right up onto a landing area that went the whole way 'round. My eyes spotted a study in a room to the right and an enormous living room off left that led outside to a veranda area and then out back to the kitchen, which was like a restaurant kitchen.

Classical music played, and I started to think they'd be waiting for me, drinking wine and eating liver pâté and waiting to murder me like some creepy horror movie.

"Alex? Is that you?"

I followed the voice through to the living room, which had these old sofas like something from the palace of Versailles. He even had bits of rug hanging from the walls instead of paintings. Fuzzy stood to welcome me. He was drinking orange juice from a champagne glass and a piece of pulp had somehow become lodged in his lovely moustache.

"Hi, Alex. Sorry, we are a little slow moving this morning."

I couldn't stop staring at the orange piece in his moustache. He must have noticed but didn't rush none to do anything about it, just kept talking all casual and smoothly wiped his mouth with a nice linen handkerchief.

"Are you thirsty?"

He placed his glasses on the coffee table. "Sabrina?" he called. A beautiful Asian woman came through holding a glass of water and a glass of juice.

"Water or juice?" she asked.

"Water is fine."

She handed me the water and proceeded to take a long drink of juice. She then kissed Fuzz, and he put his arm 'round her.

"This is my wife, Sabrina."

"Nice to meet you, Alex. I hope you guys have a nice time. Unlike you recreationists, I have to meet a client at twelve, so I'd better get moving."

"Ok, follow me," said Fuzz.

He was wearing an expensive-looking pair of sweatpants and high-tops. His hair wasn't gelled like before and was just short of falling into his eyes. On our way to his barn, we passed a crushed can of beer. He picked it up.

"This yours?"

"No sir."

We walked a couple more steps, and he put it in a trash can outside the barn door.

"My dad's," I said finally.

"You weren't joking about this family sitch, were you?"

"It's not so bad. I think we've turned the corner, you know?"

"Sure," said Fuzz sarcastically.

His barn was mostly empty but for a couple of cars covered under a hood. He had a nice piece of wood laid out on top of some old carpet under the cement. It was ten by six or so, and he had a large mirror leaning against the back wall. He had speakers attached to the wall and a stereo right by an old black leather sofa. On the opposite side of the sofa was a fridge. I wondered if this was where Fuzz and his buddies would retreat for final beers and cigars when Sabrina kicked them out for being noisy.

I warmed up real quick with some scissor jumps and knees up for like thirty seconds, followed by squats and a couple minutes stretching, during which Fuzz fingered through a round black pouch by the stereo system, picking a CD and setting it into action.

Fuzz cleared his throat, and his voice came out licorice. "Ok, Alex. Do you know any dances or just your over-two-three and sidestep?"

"Um, I guess I know all the beginner dances," I said, sweat dripping.

"Ok, let's start with the beginner reel."

"Um, I know the primary."

"Very good. Off you go."

I stood in the center of his floor and felt a little foolish. I tried to remember the steps, but they had somehow disappeared.

I started and messed up. I started a second time.

He spoke calmly. "One-two-three, two-two-three, three-two-three."

And I stood. He repeated.

"One-two-three. Come on, now."

After an awkward start, I gradually got into it and ignored the fact that he was watching me with a weird squint. Somehow as I went on, the movements became more natural.

"Ok, not bad. We have something to work with here."

He played the track, and we went over it a bunch of times. We danced side by side, and soon he started sweating. He took his sweater off, and I nearly died. The guy was built of pure muscle. His shoulders and arms were like cannons. His tee was gelled to his giant ribcage. Fuzz started getting frustrated because I was messing up what I had previously been doing flawlessly.

"Up, higher. Higher, Alex! Point up at the back. Knee. Straight. C'mon Alex, concentrate." He exhaled.

"Maybe we should take a break? My brain needs a rest."

He didn't say anything just made a moustachey face. Then he shook his head in frustration.

"No, we're trying to make a breakthrough. Let's work through it."

But his frustration played onto me. All the initial progress I had made on leaping higher and making my one-two-threes bigger had disappeared. If anything, my basics were getting worse.

Fuzz turned the music off and hummed the intro instead of rewinding the CD over and over again.

"And five, six and seven." He didn't say the eight. That annoyed me.

I started, but it was all wrong.

"No, no, no! Again. And five, six, seven."

This time I didn't dance.

"What? What now?"

"You didn't say eight."

"God!" He smacked his forehead. "You want to learn or not? I don't say the eight."

"What's the point in saying five, six, seven? Just say five, six, seven, eight. If you're going to say the numbers, say all the numbers, or else don't say them and hum. I know when to start."

"I don't think you do, because you keep losing the rhythm. You want to learn or not?"

I laughed at his bad temper. He was like a camp dragon, but a dragon nonetheless. Smoldering.

He turned his back to me and put his hand on his hip and took a couple of breaths. When he turned back 'round, he seemed to have mellowed.

"What's your real name?"

"Fran. It's short for Francis."

"Fran Anderson?"

"Yes. You can call me Fuzz, Fran, Fran Anderson or Franderson if you wish, but you can't call me anything ever again unless you start doing exactly what I'm showing you, ok?" He said it deep and abrupt and finished with a sarcastic smile.

"Ok, Fran," I drew out his name.

I started dancing again, but he raised a hand to stop me.

"You're holding back." He exhaled through rounded lips like he was about to start whistling. "Alex. Why do you want to dance?"

I thought a second. "Um, because I want to get in one of those shows when I'm older?"

"So you want to dance for money?"

"Well, yes. I mean, I guess. Like to make money to live, you know?"

He shook his head and pursed his lips.

"No, try again."

I bit my lip, not wanting to tell him the truth. He must have noticed. "Come on. No one's judging you here."

My voice came out quiet. "It helps me forget about things."

"Good. And you know why you feel better when you dance?" I shook my head yes, but he answered for me. "Because the movements make you feel good. They release endorphins. You enjoy leaping through the air, transcending time and space, the focus. You dance because you love it and it makes you happy. Not because you want to come first place in some competition or to make money. Because you're a performer, and the energy from it gives you power and happiness."

Fuzz spoke not just with his mouth and his arms but also with his eyes.

"I have an idea. What kinda music you like?"

"Um, I guess indie stuff, electronic, all sorts really."

"Do you like Flood Control?"

"I do," I said with enthusiasm.

Fuzz took out his cell phone and played one of their more electronic tracks, holding the phone in the air with one hand and clicking the beat with the fingers of his others. His head bobbed along.

"Close your eyes."

"Why?"

"Just close them. Pretend you're in a club. You want to impress some guy. Seduce him with your dancing. Dance."

I stood in one spot with my eyes closed.

"Come on, Alex. Start playing ball, or I'm not going to teach you. This song is awesome. Doesn't it make you want to dance?"

I loosened my neck and shoulders and let the rhythm take control of my body, bouncing on my toes a little and my arms doing little swimming motions.

"Good. Forget I'm here. The song is kicking off."

I danced around, moving a little more freely.

"I'm going to count you in, and I want you to dance your reel steps."

"What?" I said confused.

"No 'what'. Just do. Seduce."

And like that, on the fourth click of his fingers, I danced my Irish dance steps to one of my favorite electro songs just as the chorus came 'round, and it felt really awesome.

When the song ended, I stopped, and it was just like the lights had come up at the end of the night in a busy club, and I was sweating with excitement.

"Good, Alex. Good. That's what dancing is. It's so much fun, it makes us feel amazing. It's so natural to move to a beat." He looked at me glowingly. "You're starting to look like an Irish dancer now."

We danced for ninety minutes on and off in total.

As he drove me home, I had to ask.

"How did you get that name?"

"Well, as you can probably tell I have a bit of an issue with rage. In fact, I used to cuss a lot. In college the guys got a swear jar 'cause I couldn't stop using the f-word. They made enough money in a month to pay rent! Eventually I started saying what the fuzz, which saved me a lot of money. Then people started calling me Fuzz or Fuzzy," he said, laughing.

As we climbed my narrow mountain road, I went ahead and asked.

"So what do you think? Am I good enough to go back for this masterclass in a couple weeks?"

"Woah, really? That was your first lesson."

I didn't respond, a little disappointed by his reaction. Then I realized.

"Um, I'd like a few more lessons if that's the case. How much do you charge?"

"Ha, I hadn't really thought about it like payment in monies per se." He took his eyes off the road a moment and eye-balled me.

"What the what now?"

"You can pay me in something better than dollars. Like I mentioned before, sometimes I need dancers for entertainment purposes—in fact, we have a thing coming up soon, and I could do with some Irish dancing. It's in a retirement home."

"So you want me to dance for old people?"

"Yeah, something like that."

We got to my house, and I said thanks and goodbye, and he told me to text him during the week. I was feeling good, but the feeling was not to last.

Chapter 18

It was a delicious eighty degrees outside, but there was the iciest of atmospheres in the living room. Mom and Dad were staring silently at each other across the room, their faces tense as I entered. Mom, holding her box of pills in one hand, gave them a shake and went to the bathroom. Next thing, the toilet flushed. Mom came back in the living room and switched on the TV.

"Why did you do that, Mom?"

"Those pills make me feel like I'm on another planet. I just hate the way I feel."

I swallowed hard and looked at Dad, who was dumbfounded. He shoved his hand in his pockets and took out his keys.

"I'm going to the bar."

"Good for you," said Mom, who sat there rubbing the tattoo on her ring finger.

My stomach started cramping like crazy after that, and my queasiness was justified, because quick as you like, the screaming came a-knocking on our homestead and allowed itself to slip right in and make itself comfortable.

Lucas spent Friday and Saturday cuddling with me, and soon we had a spare bed in our room. I tried not to listen. Some of the times Mom argued and shouted to no one because Dad would take off. On Monday morning, I woke up to find the mattress all wet. Lucas looked all pale and guilty and full of resentment and embarrassment when he woke. I felt terrible.

All I did was dance and dance and hope it wasn't true, but I knew I'd have to tell Grandpa. Poor old Grandpa had the saddest face when I told him what was what. You could tell he wanted to die and the only thing stopping him was his regard for our safety. He wasn't allowed to rest in peace and instead just had ill health.

"Grandpa, I think it's time Lucas and I come live with you."

Grandpa didn't say anything, just grabbed his hat and car keys and drove off.

I texted Michelle, wanting to go to her place for some comfort, but she was busy with a 'new' friend. Then I texted Fuzz to arrange another lesson for that coming Thursday.

Mom was drinking more than ever and was in full-on rampage mode. She didn't try starting on me, but a couple of times I caught her scolding Lucas, who would hardly leave the bedroom anymore. When he did leave the house, he and Harper would wander for hours amongst the trees. Mom would then get real worried about him and send Dad or me to look for him. He was never all too far away, just wanted to be by himself.

On Tuesday Grandpa called by and took us for a drive. We went to the Child Protection Services office in Leitchfield. He must have made us an appointment, because we didn't have to wait in the reception long before a mister in a suit brought us into his office and asked Lucas and me hundreds of questions. He wrote notes and hemmed and hawed every now and again. I was feeling real excited, trying not to smile at the thought of something new about to happen, but at the end, he called Grandpa in and told us that they were so underserviced it could take a couple months before they could send a team out to the house. That put me right on edge.

Grandpa told Lucas and I not to mention any of it to Mom or Dad, but when we got home and Mom was arguing with Dad, I almost felt like telling them the game was up. Instead I went outside on the porch steps and listened to the sounds of the night. I tapped my heels on the flaking gray patio wood beneath me for a long time and tried to think of nothing.

Those following days, I danced for hours. I had two sessions a day—an hour after breakfast and forty-five minutes after lunch, more if I was able. In the evening, Lucas and I went on long bike rides. We were both so exhausted we almost had no trouble falling asleep despite everything going on.

Every night before sleep, I replayed my encounter with Kal McGettigan and repeated his positive words to myself. I needed to go to that masterclass.

Grandpa drove Lucas and I to Fuzzy's house for my next dance class.

Fuzz stared for the briefest of seconds when we both got out of the car before smiling quickly. He whistled a tune and shuffled off.

"Sa-bri-na?" he called up the stairs, before heading for the basement.

Sabrina came halfway down the stairs. "What's up?"

Fuzz's muffled voice rose like a wisp of smoke from the basement, barely audible. "…That old train set… You got me one Christmas? Know where it is?"

Sabrina's brain was busy, one finger on her delicate cheek, thumb on chin. She spied Lucas, and her eyes grew with delight. "Oh hello," she said quietly, then rushed toward the basement. "I think I do."

I felt so pleased that Fuzz was going out of his way to accommodate Lucas. "Oh, you're so warm and Fuzzy, Fuzz." I smiled sarcastically.

"Watch it," he said with fake seriousness. "It may not last."

I must have been sighing and making faces as I tied my soft shoes, because Fuzz interjected. He spoke softly.

"Anything you want to talk about?"

"Not really. I was just thinking maybe you could give me more advanced steps to work on? This stuff is getting a little tiresome."

Fuzz scrunched his face. "I don't know, Alex. I mean your flexibility is good and your turn-out is neat, nice elevation. We're making good progress with your basics, but still, your rhythm—"

I cut him off. "But Fuzz…"

He stopped himself and stared at my feet, scratching his eyebrow.

"Things bad, huh?" I pouted. "Your grandpa seems like a nice man. You don't think you guys could live with him a while?"

My voice was sad. "We're waiting for Child Protection…They said it could take months."

Fuzz nodded sympathetically. "I wish I could help."

"But you are. This," I said, pointing to the dance floor. "This helps my brain."

He fixed his moustache, combing from middle to right then middle to left with his index finger.

"Fuzz, I need new steps and more lessons. The way it is won't cut it…"

He frowned. "Actually, I have some bad news about that, straight off. I'm gonna be out of town next week; business stuff just came up."

"What?" I exclaimed. "Well, that's it, you better show me everything I'm gonna need today."

Fuzz sighed. "That's not a good idea, but whatever. Did you bring your heavy shoes? Can you rally?"

I nodded twice.

"Put them on. I'll teach you a heavy jig. Actually, I'd better go straight into hornpipe if you want to go back…"

The first thing he did was dance it through, and I recorded it on my phone. Then he spent the rest of the hour going through it with me.

"You have to hit the ground harder if you want to move your foot faster." I tried again, but he stopped me.

"No, it's not ral-ly-one. It's rally." He said the word quickly. "Real quick movement."

We practiced and practiced, but I was having a hard time getting it right. I was learning how to click, small ones, and big clicks above my head. At the end of the hour, I felt deflated, but Fuzz smiled.

"No question, Alex. You have real potential," he said, his eyes glistening. "Let's see how we go over the next couple weeks, but one thing's for sure, you better learn the value of patience. You're working great. That's gonna have to do it for today. Let's get you home. I gotta pack and take Sabri out for dinner."

Sabrina and Lucas had been playing with the train set for hours, then had made milkshakes in the blender with ice cream, syrup and ice cubes. Lucas got in the back seat and looked like he was ready to nap.

On the drive home, Fuzz told me that he would need me before he took off.

"Next week is that retirement party I told you about, and the good news is you're providing the entertainment."

Mortified, I covered my face with both hands. "Oh god. I'm not sure I'm ready for this."

"You'll be fine. And here's something else. If you do go back to Cleveland, you're going to need money. I have work you can do. I'll pay you."

"What?"

"I need help in my office. We have boxes of files that need to be categorized, and frankly, it's a pain in the butt. I'll pay you ten bucks an hour on top of the free dance lessons."

My eyes lit up. "Wow, really? That's awesome, man!"

"My pleasure, Alex."

Chapter 19

Tuesday evening Fuzz and his six-series Audi picked me up to go to a retirement function for some dude who ran a nursing home. It was being held in the strangest place I could think of — a bowling alley.

"Fuzz, what the heck is this?" I asked as we walked in to find a bunch of eighty-year-old men and women stiffly picking up and rolling balls down two open lanes. There were dentured smiles to crack cameras this way and that. There was a table set up with finger food and punch and maybe a couple of bottles of wine and whatnot.

Fuzz brought me into a back room and handed me a dress bag.

"This should fit. Warm up a bit first, ok?"

"Sure, what do you want me to dance?"

"Just dance your reel. And use your arms like they do in *Passion*. You know that goofy almost-ballet arm movement stuff? My friend Steve will be here in a while. He'll play accordion."

Fuzz left me to get ready, and after scissor jumping a couple minutes and stretching I unzipped the dress bag. Out came the most emerald green with vomit yellow shamrock patterns. It was long past my knees. I clasped my hand over my mouth, feeling dizzy and nauseous. Fuzz was right, the damn thing fit, and I was glad there wasn't a mirror to check myself.

Tentatively, I went in search of Fuzz. He chomped down on his bottom lip.

"Check yoself before you wreck yoself, Irish." He laughed. I punched him in the bicep just right, and he squealed and rubbed it better.

"Did you deliberately pick this piece of crap?"

"Wow, feisty Irish," he continued. "This is how it works. We give the stereotypers what they want."

Soon Steve arrived, a stout man in his late forties. We stood around as the olds made speeches and the guy who was retiring was presented with a plaque and a piece of crystal. Finally, it was time to dance. I was thankful it wasn't a heavy shoe dance, 'cause I had to dance on the hardwood floor and it was so slippery.

Steve was a real nice accordion player, and he knew how to get me going. I was nervous at first, and he must have noticed, but all he said was, "Don't worry. Even if you fall and break your ass, these guys are like goldfish: they'll have forgotten ten seconds later. And keep that in mind afterwards when they ask you if they've tipped."

He winked and started playing, and I had to rally myself to start, trying to swallow my laughter. I danced my primary reel and actually stopped dancing, but Steve kept playing, so I had to shuffle my feet really quickly and dance it again. When it came to the end the second time 'round, I glanced at Steve who seemed to have no intention of stopping, so I quickly started dancing the beginner reel for a while, starting to get real tired and hot under the dumb dress. Two more times I had to improvise, and just when I thought that would be an awesome cruel way to kill someone, by having them dance themselves to death, Steve winked at me, and we finished together. I was super relieved.

The olds really enjoyed my dancing, and it felt so nice to see them smiling and clapping.

We stood around chatting for another half hour before saying goodbye, and Fuzz drove me home.

"See, Alex, there's always a career in dancing for you, whether it be with Kal McGettigan or *Passion* or whatever. If you love it, you can do it. You don't have to be a champion, you just have to enjoy it, and I can see that you do."

As he pulled up at my house, he said. "Drop by my office tomorrow and I'll run through the work I've left you, ok?"

***

The next day, I cycled to Fuzzy's office, and he showed me how to file his papers before he left town. It was real tedious — filing articles and documents concerning arts bursaries in Kentucky from 1984-86 and looking for matching receipts. There were hundreds of packed white-cardboard boxes.

But in a funny way, it was actually a godsend. For three successive days, temperatures in Alderhill hit a hundred degrees. Two of those days, I brought Lucas with me, and he watched cartoons on Fuzz's laptop in the icy cool office as I worked.

Organizing the arts bursaries reminded me of what Kal had said about the Dance Teachers Commemorative Union. I had been practicing hard and believed I was making progress. I had a good feeling Fuzz would be pleased, so I decided, with time on the short side, to go ahead and apply for the money I would need. I used his office phone and made some calls.

The secretary of the Commemorative Union told me that I could apply for a grant of up to three hundred dollars if I had a special letter from my dance teacher. I emailed Kal McGettigan's work address, and the very next day, there was a letter waiting for me to print out. It read, *I, Kal McGettigan, request that Alexandra Maslow be provided with the maximum sum of three hundred dollars in order to attend a masterclass of Irish dancing and thus further her professional development.*

I was so proud. It meant that I only needed to get another couple hundred bucks together. I posted my application the following day. Fuzzy's secretary clocked me in and out every day, and by the time Fuzz came back, I had worked roughly twenty hours.

I had been working relentlessly on my hornpipe. But practicing without a teacher was frustrating. The masterclass in Cleveland consumed my mind 24/7. School was back on the twenty-fourth of August, and the masterclass was the week before. I had less than two weeks to get things right.

Having to see Vinnie again also played on my mind. Dad came and watched me with admiring eyes during one of my episodes of dance rage, and I ended up punching him in the arm and spilling his beer.

I was nervous yet excited to see Fuzzy that Saturday and hoping beyond hope he was as pleased as I was with my development.

Chapter 20

That Saturday Dad drove me to Fuzz's, and I met him in his barn.

"You want me to dance the beginner reel and the slip-jig?"

He batted away my question with a look of disgust. "No, forget that."

I raised my eyebrows. "But I think I got them real good." My voice trailed.

"Yeah, I'm sure," he said in a way that made me feel dumb. "Let's see the hornpipe."

I changed into my heavy shoes, heart pounding with excitement so much so my fingers fumbled as I struggled to tie my laces.

"Breathe, Alex," he said calmly, and knelt down to finish the job for me.

He pressed play on the CD player, pointed to the center of the floor and counted me in without words. I had worked hours on the new steps since the last time I saw him and felt excited and hopeful. I danced around him, holding my head high, face relaxed while he nodded his head and tapped his foot. He paused the CD as the tune ended. I smiled with my eyebrows raised.

"Not bad, Alex. It's a good start," he said in his usual baritone voice. He ran his hand through his hair as his gaze elongated.

"Huh? Fuzz? What do you mean? Can I go or not?" He didn't answer.

I swallowed. "Fuzz, you think I'm good enough to go to the masterclass?"

"How many weeks do we have?"

"Like eight days?"

He pressed his lips tight. "Alex, I'm really sorry." My shoulder dropped, deflated. A rush of disappointed blood swam into my face. "I believe you need to keep working on the basics. There's no benefit going to an advanced workshop at your stage of development."

"Jesus, Fuzz," I yelled. "I'm breaking my ass and all and I feel like...I don't know. You do realize you have to make me a World Champion like, ASAP? I mean I got to get in this show, I have to get picked. I have to get me and Lucas out of this position..." I was shaking hard all over.

He exhaled. "Alex, please." He steadied my arm. "Stop this. Use your logic. You're a complete beginner, and you're fifteen." He sighed before continuing in a computerized tone. "I should have started you off with a jig. I thought because we were in a rush and all...But hopefully it proves a point—you have to put in the time. The basics...This stuff takes time. Plus I owe you a hundred and fifty dollars, and you need...two hundred or more, on top of the bursary? Then you gotta pay for the bus and food and everything else in between? And what about your brother? Are you planning on bringing him or leaving him in that trailer with those two psychos? I mean, Alex, it's just not worth that investment at this point."

I grunted, my entire body tensing.

"You can go if you want, I'm not your father. But if you go and don't perform well, you risk being crossed off Kal's watch-list, and you don't want to give him a reason to make that definitive call."

Fuzz must have noticed how upset I looked.

"Your light shoe dancing is very nice. Your legs are strong, your leaps are awesome and you command the eye. You can kick above your head, which looks fantastic. I can see why Kal said positive things. But you have got to park this complete fantasy you've created. You're not getting in any show. Not now, and not in the next three years. I hate to be this blunt. I had crazy fantasies too when I was a dumb teenager."

"Ouch," I said.

"Sorry, I didn't mean that you're dumb. It's just such a teen thing to do…This unrealistic dream stuff."

"Dreams can come true," I whispered.

"Ok, I'm not going to argue with that. Let's keep this positive. You've only been learning for what, six weeks?"

I stared at the ground and mustered a quiet, "Since May, I guess."

He started clapping with total sincerity.

"I'm so impressed. When you give yourself a moment to reflect, Alex, you can feel proud and optimistic. Right now, we need to get you competing…Cover the syllabus and climb the ladder. You need to keep working for me, 'cause feiseanna aren't cheap. They are like thirty to fifty dollars a pop. How's that?"

"I guess," I said quietly.

"Alex, you have something that people can't learn, that is unmeasurable. When I look in your eyes, I can see you can be something special."

That gave me the chills.

"Competitions will be kicking off when school starts. You need stage experience. Dancing in this barn in front of me is easy, but you need to build other important skills. You don't know how big and bright these competitions get. You have to graduate from this beginner material before you're allowed to learn more complex steps and work your way up the chain. I should have started you off with a treble jig, but we may as well push through now with this hornpipe."

And that's what we did for the next hour. Worked and worked on getting my hornpipe right.

On the drive home, I reflected. It was pretty tough to swallow. Dreams made people crazy. It was a matter of controlling the pace of the dream.

Chapter 21

My anxiety grew out of control as I thought about the torment we would undergo at home as we waited for Child Protection to get their asses in gear. Lucas was constantly struggling with his breathing, and I had to take Tylenol every day to help with a persistent headache. But one day, I had an idea of how to speed things along. It all happened after a tough dance session. I ran a bath, and not wanting to waste the hot water, I called Lucas. As he soaked and played with some toys, I noticed a purple bruise no more than the size of a plum on his back just above his butt.

"How did that happen?" He looked at me, guilty, without answering. "Did Mom hit you? Was it Dad?"

He shook his head no. And just like that, a plan formed, but right as I was about to act on it, my phone rang. It was Fuzz.

"Hey, I'm close to your place. You home? I need you for an hour or two."

I looked at Lucas playing in the water and at his bruise and exhaled quietly.

"Yeah, I'm free."

"Ok. See you in fifteen."

"I'll meet you outside."

I washed Lucas up quick and dried him off, then went outside, where Fuzz was parked waiting.

We drove south towards his house.

"There's a small feis in Arlington on Saturday."

"Saturday?" I yelped. He nodded. "Don't I have to be registered with a dance school or something? I don't even have a dress or a wig or anything. How am I gonna get there?"

"I can enter you as an independent dancer. I have a meeting out there Saturday, so I can take you."

"You think I'm ready for a feis?" I asked as he parked up and we made our way inside his home. He ignored me and kissed Sabrina, who had a milkshake moustache.

"Yum," he said.

Ew." I squealed. "Get a room!"

They both laughed.

"Sabrina, c'mere."

He made us stand back to back. Looking at Sabrina, I had thought we were kinda the same height, but I was wrong.

"Alex, you have at least three inches on her. Guess you won't be wearing her old dress," said Fuzz.

"You used to dance?" I yelped.

"Sure did. I was in *Passion* during a year out of college."

"Wow! What was it like?"

Her face said it all.

"Sabri, can you check to see if you still have that old wig that Darla left behind?"

She went and checked and came back with an empty box. "I think the dog ate it."

I looked around. There was no sign of a dog.

Sabrina had a habit of squinching her button nose when deep in thought. "Ok, so we don't have a dress, we don't have a wig, but we have soft and heavy shoes, right?" I nodded. "Poodle socks?"

I nodded the opposite way.

She shuffled off and came back with a couple pairs of poodle socks. She grabbed her car keys off the counter top. "Ok, let's go to Walmart."

Shopping with Sabrina was fun but fast. I wanted to ask her all about *Passion,* but she was focused. She picked out this itzy black skirt and found a black leotard to match. My face elongated, and I said no way, but she dragged me into the changing rooms. The skirt barely covered my thighs.

"My butt, Sabrina. You can see my butt!" I protested.

"Don't worry, I have sports shorts you can wear."

The outfit cost less than twenty bucks, and even though I felt so self-conscious when I looked in the mirror, there was a comforting gaze emanating from Sabrina.

"You look like a woman," she said.

Afterwards Fuzzy dropped me home. "Maybe it's time I met your parents."

"No way, Fuzz. Not happening."

But he insisted and parked the car and got out after me. "Don't you think your teacher should meet the prodigy's parents?"

The screen door slammed shut as Mom came out onto the porch.

"Is this the mister who teaches you dance?" asked Mom, slurring.

"Yeah, Mom, this is Mr. Anderson."

Fuzz smiled. "Your daughter is very talented, Mrs. Maslow. You should be very proud."

Mom gulped and spilled beer and wiped her mouth on her tanned arm. Her eyes were wobbling 'round her sockets. "Oh, she shouldn't waste her time on that."

I tried to stay calm. "But Mom, didn't Grandma love to dance? And she used to sing Irish to you when you were young. You told me that before."

"Oh, she did, I guess. But she knew better than to get her hopes up none. You shouldn't either."

She fished around in her pockets for a box of cigarettes and lit one up before walking down the field to talk to Roly.

"I'm proud of you, Alex. Keep it up," said Fuzz softly before leaving. "See you tomorrow."

That night with all the excitement, I found it hard to sleep. Saturday would be my first ever competition. Lucas got in beside me, and I remembered I had totally forgotten about the bruise and my plan. And I pushed it out of my mind. It could wait a day. Right then all I wanted to do was think about dance.

Chapter 22

Arlington was a two-hour drive. We got take-out coffee and muffins to eat on the way. Fuzz was back in his usual three-piece, glasses resting on his head; his hair had more grease than a Wendy's fryer. We talked a little, but then he listened to politics on the radio, and my eyes got sleepy.

I woke as we pulled up to the high school where the feis was being held, feeling refreshed after a poor night's sleep. It was so hot and still only eight AM. It was the first feis after summer and crowded with eager parents and children all wearing layers of tan, and with all the wigs and fancy dresses and all, it was just like I remembered.

Fuzz couldn't stay. He registered me as an independent dancer, and I coughed up a whole bunch of money. It was a fifteen-buck entry fee, then another ten for the beginner reel, light-jig, slip-jig, single jig and hornpipe. Sixty-five bucks down the flusher in crap-hole Arlington before I had even danced a step. It was tough to swallow.

"See you later, Alex. Don't worry, and try to enjoy yourself. I'll be back in two hours." He kissed me on the cheek, waved hi to some old dolls, then left.

The school gym had three different stages laid out. There were dozens of tiny beginners dancing, and that was taking an age. They danced three at a time. A better idea would have been to line all hundred of them up and have a judge stand beside them with a megaphone. After letting them all dance a bit, the judge could shout at the girls who were no good to get off the stage until there were only ten left. It would have eliminated a bunch of unnecessary waiting around and watching terrible beginners. Plus, it would really test out their stamina. I'm sure some moms would bring their exhausted kids home afterwards and feel real thankful. But my good humor soon disappeared when it was time for me to get ready.

I got changed in the bathroom and found a quiet space down a hallway where I could warm up. I hated being there alone. I wanted to text Kate, but I had left my phone in Fuzzy's car. I felt super self-conscious when I went back into the gym. My hair wasn't long enough to tie up, so I pinned it back to keep it falling into my eyes.

I couldn't really tell who the other girls in my category were. I asked an organizer, and she showed me where I should line up. There were two others waiting — a girl with really bad acne and braces and a boy. The girl was real polite.

"Hey. Your outfit is cute."

"Thanks," I said, wanting to go home.

"Is it your first time?"

I nodded.

"Well, my advice is to enjoy it, because it's really lots of fun. My mom's dying wish was for me to become an Irish dancer. She was from County Mayo in Ireland and always wanted a daughter who danced, but I was never interested, so after she got sick I swore to make her proud."

"Oh," I said, feeling bad.

She was grinning with a mouth full of metal. Then she gently punched my arm. "I'm just kidding. My mom's not sick or dying or even dead for that matter. I've been dancing for about a year. I'm no good, but I really enjoy it."

Somehow her whack story helped put my mind at ease, until she quickly followed with, "Anyways, we're up."

"We are?"

"Yeah."

"How does this even work?"

"There are three beginners in our age group, so they'll make us stay on stage and dance all the light shoe dances one after another."

I followed her onto the stage, and she pointed at where I should stand. I was trying to figure out which dance came first, but the keyboard started immediately, and I stood there confused. It felt like everyone was staring at me, and eventually they were, because the other two started dancing and I was standing there staring at the keyboard guy. Thankfully, the judge rang a bell, and the music stopped. I stayed where I was, and the other two lined up again.

"It's the beginner reel," she said.

I closed my eyes a bit and took a long, slow inhale and exhale just like I told Kate all those times. And over and over again, I just said quietly to myself, "Alex, you got this."

The music started up again, and this time I danced like I had for Fuzzy and in my garage. I was dancing in my first ever feis, and it was over quicker than it had started. I had really only started enjoying it by the final few bars. My face hurt from smiling as I felt this strange kind of euphoria. The girl looked across at me as we went back to our starting positions and the announcer called Beginner One Light Jig.

"Wow, you're a really nice dancer."

"Thanks."

"Patricia," she said, smiling.

"Alex," I replied.

Then we danced our light jig. I was feeling a lot better about things now. I stayed to the left-hand side of the stage, not wanting to be too adventurous, whereas Patricia crisscrossed all over the place. She knew the steps but didn't really have any rhythm.

I kept wondering to myself as I danced why-oh-why was there a guy dancing with us. He was quite good despite being a little chubby.

Within a matter of minutes, we had finished all our light shoe rounds and had fifteen minutes to get a drink and change into our heavies.

The chubby kid had excellent heavy footwork. I danced all my beginner dances except a traditional set, which I did not have.

We waited an hour, then it was time to go to the back stage for the announcer to call our results. I was ridiculously nervous even though there were only about six people hanging around waiting. I had to try so hard not to scream when the announcer called out my number. I came first in all the light shoe rounds. Patricia could see I was trying to contain my happiness.

"Go on, Alex. Let it out," I screamed in her face and almost crushed her with a hug.

Fuzz quick marched towards me as the announcer called the results of the hornpipe.

"How did you dance?" he whispered. He spied my medals and winked.

"Good."

The announcer said "First in hornpipe, Number 141, Joseph Daly."

I looked at Fuzz, and his mouth fell open and closed a couple times like a fish.

"What the what, Alex? I thought by bringing you here, we could move you along quickly because of the low numbers competing."

But I was just laughing my ass off. Fuzzy didn't see the funny side.

"Come on, Fuzz. You didn't see him. He was really good."

"Really good at eating Big Macs? Jebus!"

But I put my hand up and shushed him. "Let me just check something real quick."

I ran over to the announcer and checked to see what score I got. She told me it was over eighty, and I knew that meant I could advance to Beginner Two. But Fuzz shook his head, unimpressed.

"Come on. Let's get out of here. I wanna get back to my wife."

Chapter 23

I climbed the steps to my house, clenching my medals, unable to stop grinning. I hadn't even opened the door when I heard yelling in the living room. Dad was sitting on the couch wearing nothing but shorts, watching baseball, ignoring Mom's screams for him to change the channel. I stood at the doorway and hung the medals 'round my neck, hoping they would notice, but Mom just went 'round pulling up cushions, looking for the remote control, Dad covering his ears with both hands. Finally, Mom screamed almighty, and her face went all red. She picked up the TV, tugged the wire clean out of the wall, shoved her way past me and dropped it outside with a smash in the front yard.

I stared wide-eyed at her as she marched back inside. Dad got up, grabbed his car keys and left.

"Well, lookie here, if it ain't Miss Champion Dance Queen and her precious medals."

I grabbed a bag of potato chips and went in the bedroom. Lucas lay on the bed with a coloring book.

"What you got there, 'round your neck?" he asked softly.

But the words didn't register. I sat on my bed, staring into space.

"Alex? Where d'you get those?"

"Oh, these? I won them at an Irish dancing competition today."

He nodded. "Can I see?" His voice was rasping badly.

"Sure." I took them off, and he fingered them with one eye closed, like some kind of scientist. I searched the drawers for his inhaler and gave it a shake. It was empty. I sat him on my knee.

"You must be pretty good, winning first place, but I got bad news for you," he said, solemnly handing me back my medals.

"Oh yeah?"

"Those are fake gold. Those people cheated you, and I know it ain't fair, but everything's not always fair."

"Oh, ok," I said.

"Wanna see my medal?"

"Sure."

He took off his sneaker, and a tarnished old coin fell out.

"I keep it in there for safe-keeping and good luck."

As he bent over to untie his shoe, I saw the bruise on his lower back once more and remembered. He sat back up on my knee and snuggled his little head under my chin.

"That's nice you have that. It will bring us good luck, you know."

I closed my eyes and sighed and rocked him and felt a weight of sadness and pain pressing down on me. We would never be happy. It was time.

"Lucas, remember how we used to play pretend? I have a game that is so much fun, like doctors and nurses. Wanna play?"

We roleplayed for maybe twenty minutes. Then I got ready. With some makeup, I painted a purple-colored bruise on my arm. I fed Lucas an apple, and soon we were ready to cycle into town. Mom was lying on the couch. I took the last twenty from her purse, then we sneaked off to Alderhill's medical center.

"You remember everything I said?" I asked as we locked up our bikes at the rack.

He nodded. "Alex, I'm scared."

"Don't be. It's just like we practiced."

We waited and waited, and soon my heart thumped like crazy, like I was having a heart attack, but Lucas played with some toys and even made a new friend to keep him company. I was tapping my foot so much so that other patients started to fidget too. I guess nervousness was contagious.

Finally, we were called. His name was Dr. Peters. He had a young, tan face with totally white hair and black eyebrows.

"Miss, how can I help you today?"

"Sir," I started. And I was so scared. "Sir, it's my mom and dad. They've been abusing us." But the words didn't even seem real to me. I found it hard to speak with an honest air. I felt like a great big fraud.

"They drink a lot. And they fight. And sometimes they...They get physical."

"With each other."

I nodded.

"And with you."

I nodded once more.

"And my grandpa, we already talked to Child Protection, but they've not done anything, and it's been months…"

I lifted Lucas off my lap. "Are you ready?"

"I don't wanna, Alex."

Dr. Peters spoke softly to Lucas. "Tell me about your mom and dad."

"Their name's is Debby and Dad, and we live in a trailer. We have a horse." Lucas kept looking down at the floor and took some extra coaxing. Finally, we got him to lift his shirt, and the doctor examined his bruise.

"How did this happen?"

But Lucas wouldn't speak even though we had rehearsed it over and over.

"Anything else you want to tell me, Lucas?"

"Momma used to buy me Toasted Oats, but she doesn't no more."

He made him stand on the weighing scales.

"So what do you eat now?"

"Chewing gum. Except I'm not supposed to."

The doctor asked him to wait outside so he could talk to me.

"Does your mom ever get physical with you?"

I nodded and removed my cardigan and showed him my upper arm.

"How did this happen?"

"Um, she punched me."

"Why?"

"We were arguing...There was no food, and we were starving, and they were so drunk and shouting."

Finally, he exhaled. "Alex, although Lucas's bruise may indeed be genuine, yours is clearly not," he said, rubbing black makeup between his thumb and forefinger. "Lucas may have gotten that bruise falling off a bike or something." He sat back down across from me and looked deep into my eyes, which wavered back and forth and soon became blurry as the silence roared.

The first droplet took the longest to fall, but after that, I was inconsolable. He handed me a tissue and typed on his computer for minutes on end as I cried silently.

"I don't know what to believe, Ms. Maslow."

"I'm telling you the truth, you have to believe me," I said, sobbing. "We even had to call the cops the other night, just check the records."

He rubbed his tongue up against his upper teeth. "I'm going to call Child Protection directly and ask if they can upgrade your case to urgent—see if they can send some people over to talk with your parents. That's the best I can do."

It rained on our bike ride home. We sneaked in the back door and went straight to our room. I hoped Mom and Dad wouldn't come check on us, because they'd find we had the old TV. Lucas and I watched Pixar movies, but I couldn't relax, my mind summersaulting.

Before dark, the iPad buzzed. Kate Face-Timed, wanting to know everything about the feis, and laughed so hard when I told her the boy beat me.

She had just had her second operation on the week of her double-digit birthday, which she was so excited about. The doctors broke her leg again so as it could heal the same length as the other. That almost made me puke. The doctors said it was a successful operation, and that she would wear an 'alien's army boot'. Kate was excited, but it sounded pretty rough to me. Before she said goodbye, she said she wished I was in Lakewood right now at Kal McGettigan's masterclass. She said she saw pictures on Instagram and it looked like so much fun.

I wished she hadn't reminded me. Having expended every emotion known to mankind in the space of twenty-four hours, I fell asleep, drained and void of any feeling.

Chapter 24

The following night, Dad missed dinner. Two of Mom's friends came over, and they took to singing and drinking the night away. Somehow Lucas slept, but I was frustrated and antsy and a little sick to my stomach. To make matters worse, I had made the mistake of looking up Facebook pics of Kal McGettigan's masterclass. Jessica Harvey was in the forefront of most of the photos, wearing the skimpiest tee known to mankind.

I threw my phone on the ground and covered my ears as the singing reached new volumes. I lay there wondering how long it would take Child Protection to send a team out. I thought about recording everything on my phone as evidence for when they finally showed up.

After a while, I heard Mom's friends leave, and the quiet was eerie. A little later, I heard Dad's car pull into the driveway at speed, followed by quick footsteps. Then silence. Ten minutes later, the front door slammed. Dad spoke in a voice I hadn't heard before. It wasn't loud or angry or anything, it was just different. I crept out to the hall to listen.

"Debby, now why you have to go and do that now, huh? I can't believe you did that to Alex's studio."

Studio? What in the hell was Dad talking about? I laced up my sneakers quickly, ran out the back door to the barn and switched on the light. My dance floor was all black and ash and dust and wet with bits of hay lying unburnt here and there. I figured Dad must have extinguished it. The mirror was smashed into thousands of glowing pieces scattered all 'round the wooden floor.

I ran back inside as quiet as I could and looked into the kitchen. Mom was holding family photos and a lighter, burning them one by one. She had this shit-eating grin on her face and didn't say a word, just allowing the burning paper to fall onto the tiles before starting on the next photo. It was Lucas as a newborn baby. Her smile was the same. *Critch* went the sound of the lighter. Dad's eyes filled with tears. My brain was screaming and thumping and throbbing.

Dad wept quietly and went in his bedroom. He came back out, his wallet bulging in his back pocket. Mom mumbled, incomprehensible. Dad didn't say anything, just stepped outside. I didn't hear the car start up but saw the lights swinging 'round the corner and out onto the dirt road. Mom kept on talking to herself and burning pictures. I slipped into the living room quickly and called Grandpa.

"Grandpa, come quick." That's all I said. Then I called the cops.

I waited a few minutes at the window, searching for a light or listening for the sound of a car, and with Dr. Wallace's final words ringing in my ears, I went in the kitchen, hoping my timing was right.

"Hey, Debby!" I shouted. She turned around, startled. "You good for nothing hick! I can't believe I came out of you."

She inhaled sharply a couple times and blinked over and over as she tried to sober up. She brushed sticky hair from her face. I continued towards her real slow. My voice quivered at first.

"You are the nothing but a useless redneck, a dumb alcoholic. Nobody loves you, Debby, not Dad, not me, not Lucas." Her eyes flickered at the sound of Lucas's name. She stumbled a little toward me. I latched onto her fear.

"That's right. Lucas is terrified of his own momma. You know why? 'Cause you're a good-for-nothing, stale piece of crap, Debby! You can rot in hell. I'm taking Lucas away; you'll never see him again."

A car pulled up outside, and I knew it was make or break time. I picked up a bottle and smashed it off the counter top. Then I advanced.

"You gonna try and hurt me, Debby? Here, go on now. Take this. Come on at me." I rolled the broken bottle toward her and hoped she would pick it up just as the cops walked in. I wanted her to attack me and for the cops to witness it all. She didn't move, so I shoved her just a little, not wanting her drunken ass to fall over and not be able to get up again. She didn't retaliate. I shoved her again and again until she was against the refrigerator, using it to keep her upright.

"Come on, Debby."

But Mom just started crying like a child and mumbling I don't know what. I grabbed her by the shoulders and shook her. She wouldn't fight back. She wouldn't shove me back. Grandpa came running in. He was red in the face, and I kept yelling at Mom, not even knowing what I was saying. Grandpa started pulling me away as I threatened her and called her every name I knew. But Mom just cried quietly and mumbled how sorry she was.

"I'm sorry, Alex. I love you."

The more she said those words, the more I wanted to hurt her. Grandpa wheezed hard as he pulled me back. The front door burst open, and the two cops from the previous night came running in. The male cop caught Mom and turned her sharply against the fridge and cuffed her. Just as that happened, Grandpa's grip on me weakened, and he made a funny noise. I turned 'round, and he was clutching his chest, one knee on the ground.

"Grandpa? Grandpa, what's the matter?"

He closed his eyes and fell backwards onto the cold white tiles.

"Officer, officer, quick," I yelled. The lady cop turned 'round. "There's something wrong with Grandpa."

She ran over and tended to him, putting her ear against his mouth and checking his pulse. The male cop, with one arm 'round Mom, pulled out his walkie and called for an ambulance. Mom started screaming and thrashing like a great white, and the officer needed all his strength to hold on to her. The lady cop started doing chest compressions on Grandpa, and that went on for what seemed like hours until she got his heart beating again.

Grandpa kinda woke but couldn't keep his eyes open. Lucas watched quietly from the kitchen door, face gray, teddy bear in his hand. Finally, the male cop dragged Mom out into the patrol car.

It seemed to take the paramedics forever to arrive. When they did, they put a breathing tube down Grandpa's throat and wired him up to some machines.

I tried getting a hold of Dad, but when I called, his cell rang on the living room coffee table. The cops wouldn't let Lucas and I stay at home by ourselves. I wasn't sure if we should go to the hospital with Grandpa. Part of me was too frightened to go, and I didn't want Lucas witnessing none of it either. We were all so scared.

"Is there anyone else you can call?" the male cop asked.

"Yes," I said, and dialed Fuzzy's number.

I was shaking so hard. I went to Lucas and held him tight. They took Grandpa in the ambulance. Both officers stayed with us until Fuzz arrived, wearing his pajamas and a t-shirt. He came sprinting up the steps and came straight over and hugged me.

"Alex, what happened? Are you alright?"

I started crying and couldn't sound a word. "Come on you two, into the car."

He exchanged details with the officer, and soon we were in Fuzz's home, trying to relax. I wanted to go to the hospital, but Fuzzy told me there was no point.

The next morning, he worked from home, and as soon as I stirred, he made me some eggs and toast. Sabrina had taken the day off work and had gone to the park with Lucas, who had woken earlier. Fuzz brought me to the hospital, and we were able to find out that Grandpa had had a heart attack but was in stable condition. We weren't allowed to see him. They were getting him ready for heart bypass surgery.

I called Tammy using Fuzzy's cell and told her everything, trying to hold back the tears. Tammy could barely speak. As I handed Fuzz back his phone, I wondered what would end up happening to Lucas and me.

Chapter 25

I spent the day at the hospital. That whole time, I prayed to the universe to let Grandpa be ok. I wondered where Dad was and thought about how frightened he would be when he arrived home and none of us were there. I wondered what the cops had done with Mom. Poor Grandpa — he didn't need any of this; he deserved a peaceful retirement.

Then I thought about my part in all of this. It was all my fault. I had asked the universe to help us out, asked to go live with Grandpa, and everything had almost worked out but not the way I planned. Thoughts of Grandpa not being around to take care of Lucas and me were too much. I hated myself for thinking like that, for being so selfish.

An old lady with white hair and glasses and her temples tainted from sun damage arrived in the waiting area before three PM. Her mouth dropped open when she saw me.

"Oh my, you have your grandfather's eyes. I haven't seen you since you were a baby!"

She shook my hand. My mouth hung open.

"I'm Peggy."

"Oh, Grandpa's sister?"

"That's right. I came all the way from West Virginia this morning when I heard what happened. The doctors say he's doing fine and almost ready for the operation." I nodded. "What happened? Was he working too hard?"

I couldn't bring myself to explain anything; it was all too much. "I guess so," I mumbled.

We sat down in the waiting area, and she talked and talked. She told me all about when she and Grandpa were little, and all I had to do was listen and nod and say 'yes' every now and then. After a while, I got real tired, so I asked if she wanted coffee and felt foolish because I had to ask her for money. When I came back with our drinks, Tammy had arrived. Her eyes were dark bags, and her skin looked so tight 'round her forehead. We hugged, and she started crying.

"What happened, Alex?"

"It was Mom. Grandpa was trying to help, then he sat down real quick holding his chest."

Tammy fished a tissue out of her purse and dabbed at her eyes. "Where's your father?"

"I don't know."

The doctors urged us all to go home and get some rest because Grandpa wouldn't be ready for surgery until the following day, but some cops arrived, wanting to take a statement from me about what had happened. Soon after that, a couple of Child Protection workers arrived. Tammy and I sat in a quiet area of the cafeteria, and they documented everything.

I had to go into fine details of what life had been like over the past few years and months. Tammy clasped her hand over her mouth when she heard some of the things

I said. She cried when I told the rep how Mom burned the old photographs. I was too numb to cry, but one image stayed with me the whole time I relayed my stories. Mom's words when I was provoking her. *"I'm so sorry. I love you, Alex."* Those words haunted me. I kept those to myself.

After finishing the report, I went outside to get some air. It was frigid in the hospital and hot as hell outside. When I returned, Aunt Peggy said that Lucas and I could go and live with her. I didn't know what to say — couldn't even say thank you for the offer. That was too awful to fully comprehend. Thankfully, a few minutes later, Tammy and the Child Protection lady came. They had all agreed that it would be best for Lucas and me to go to Lakewood for the short term. The cops were placing a restraining order on Debby, and priority would go toward finding our father.

Tammy dropped us back to Fuzz's house and went back to the hospital, where she stayed until Grandpa was safely out of surgery. Lucas and I hung out at Fuzz's mansion and watched endless movies. He offered to do some dancing with me in the evening, but I sat around, listless. Michelle called a couple times wondering why I hadn't been in school, but I didn't answer, just a text to let her know how bad things were.

A couple days later, when Tammy couldn't miss any more time from work and she knew Grandpa was out of danger, Lucas and I packed a bag and were on our way back to Cleveland. Peggy had agreed to stay with Grandpa a couple weeks, until he was stronger.

I was reminded of a wildlife program I had watched one time. It was about a forest in the tropics called a mangrove forest. It was a real neat ecosystem that Mother Nature had provided for little fishies and other vulnerable animals to live in and grow up in until they were big and strong enough to tackle the bigger oceans, and where they could grow and play in safety from predators. I was hoping Lakewood would be our mangrove forest.

Chapter 26

It felt so strange walking into the Buckmans' house that night sometime between the moon going down and the sun coming up. Tammy was so gray and tired from driving and worrying. She could hardly speak and went straight in her bedroom. I didn't even try to find Lucas a place to lie, just gathered my sleepy little man in beside me in the single bed. I knew Kate was awake because she was keeping real still as we settled. But my lights were out fast. I didn't even notice Lucas getting up the following morning. I got up after midday, feeling groggy.

I grabbed a glass of water and sat with my legs folded on the couch next to Kate, who watched cartoons, her left leg in a clean white cast, which rested on a chair. Lucas sat on the mat, coloring.

"I'm so happy you're back," Kate said, smiling.

"Me too. How's your leg?"

She closed her eyes and nodded quickly. "I can feel it's a million times better."

I pulled my neck to one side then the other, and it cracked loudly. Kate looked at me like my head was about to fall off. I got up and lifted Lucas onto my knee, and we cuddled. We sat watching TV for hours on end, ignoring the calls of the glorious end-of-summer sun outside, only rising to use the bathroom and to feast on cookies and milk.

Tammy wasn't home until after five. Her eyes were puffy and dark. She had obviously worked a full day on three hours sleep. Trying to contain a yawn, she called me into the kitchen and closed the door.

"Peggy called a little while ago with an update. Apparently, your mom went wild when they issued her with a restraining order, and she spent two nights in a cell."

I silently mouthed the word 'wow'.

"Grandpa is doing fine after surgery, and they are keeping a good eye on him. But the bad news is neither the authorities nor any of the neighbors know the whereabouts of your father."

I scrunched my face. "What, why? Where would he go?"

Tammy pursed her lips. I couldn't understand how Dad could just abandon us.

"He'll probably show up drunk somewhere soon enough," I said, hopeful. But Tammy shrugged.

"I talked with the social worker. She wasn't too encouraged by your fad's disappearance. She seemed to think that even if he did show up in the next day or two, it would be wise…Well, what I'm saying is she asked me if I would hold on to you and Lucas for a little bit longer, until things settled down."

"Like until Grandpa is better?" Tammy nodded.

"Ok," I said, a little shocked. "But what if he doesn't get better?"

Tammy went to the fridge.

"We're not going to consider that right now."

"Can't we just stay here like, indefinitely?"

Tammy shook her head slowly. "Impossible."

"But why?"

"It just is. Why don't you try to relax? Things will work out."

Kate was ecstatic when I told her, but I didn't know how to feel. Would our lives always whirl around like a vicious storm?

"We can get down to some serious dance practice, Alex. We can make you a champion now."

But I wasn't in the mood for celebrating. I wanted everything to go dark for a while. I couldn't make sense of the past few weeks.

"I don't really feel like it right now."

"Oh, come on, Alex, that's no way for a champion to talk. Come on, we don't got all that much time."

I didn't answer, which only encouraged her. "And Kal said, didn't he? He's going to announce something big soon, and besides, you promised me."

To my surprise, Bailey, who had just come in from school and set her bag in her bedroom, shouted through.

"Kate, give it up now."

Kate got up and clinked toward the kitchen, her tail between her legs. Lucas was done with coloring and was engrossed in cartoons. I would explain everything to him later, after I had made sense of it. I just needed a little space. I went in the bedroom, lay down and closed my eyes.

The next day, I stayed home minding Lucas as everyone went about their school and work lives. Lucas hadn't said much since everything, and I wasn't much in the mood for finding out what was going through his brain. He didn't seem sad or scared, and his asthma wasn't playing up, so that was good enough for me. I, on the other hand, didn't know where my head was at.

Thursday night I slept so well, but that was only because I wasn't aware of Tammy's intentions. At seven the following morning, she knocked on the bedroom door and told me to get dressed for school. Too sad to argue, I soon found myself back at Miller High, starting my sophomore year with the same kids I had been with the previous winter. I didn't even have a backpack.

Nobody made a big deal of me as I joined Mr. Gonzales's English class. He nodded kindly, and I found a spot to sit and rest my head down back. Some familiar faces rolled by, smiling and saying hi. I felt so ugly with bags under my eyes and just wanted to hide. Dominique looked at me blankly. Bailey was busy flirting with a couple of dudes.

The last face my eyes fell on was Josh's. He nodded a 'hey' towards me. He was one of the reasons Bailey had hated my guts so bad last time. They had been kinda dating, but he'd had a thing for me. He had cut his hair and if possible was more handsome than ever. I didn't see Vanessa and wondered if she had moved school again.

None of this mattered. The whole time, I wondered what would happen if Grandpa wasn't strong enough to take care of Lucas and me. Where did Dad go? Would he ever come back, or had Debby driven him away from us forever? I thought about what I could do, which was basically nothing. Everything was out of my hands. The worst fear of all was that Grandpa wouldn't recover and Lucas and I would end up in some kind of home or foster care. That made me nauseous. I worked hard to get through the first day.

There had been changes to the school since my time there. The school now employed security guards that patrolled the grounds in golf carts, and they had weird nicknames like Goofy and Mobil One. All students had to carry IDs 'round their necks, and I wondered if it was anything to do with what had happened to me after I had been assaulted by Vanessa and Dominique and had left school without permission. The real reason, I later found out, was that so many kids had been sneaking home at lunchtime to smoke weed.

As I walked home after final bell on my first day with the sun hot on my back, it dawned on me that my summer was over and I had totally missed out on it. It seemed to have disappeared in a puff of smoke, with not one memory to savor.

The house was quiet. I ate a snack, and not feeling so good, went to bed, but for a long time, my brain was riddled with diseased thoughts. I thought about Mom and the anger I felt towards her, but at the back of it all, I felt so bad. I pictured her smoking on the porch, the house quiet and her probably crying, everyone she loved gone forever. I didn't want those thoughts. I hated her — she had ruined so many people's lives, yet still, she was Mom. After an hour of lying there trying to rest my brain, I must have hit an off button. Then I slept and slept. Lucas came to check on me for dinner, but I grumbled at him and he left me alone.

That weekend went by in a cloudy daze. I took Lucas to the park for a walk, and he chased after a ball as I sat under a tree staring at the sky. Sunday was hot, and I sat on the porch swing for hours and hours while Tammy took Kate and Lucas to the movies to cool down. I went to bed at six that evening, a lifeless, soulless, empty bag of bones.

On Monday morning, I woke with an almighty headache. Tammy pressed her cold palm onto my forehead, gave me some Tylenol and sent me back to bed. She was working nights, which meant she could keep an eye on Lucas.

Three more days I stayed in bed, but on Friday morning, Tammy forced me to get up. Everything was so surreal. There was something very comforting about being back in Lakewood, but deep in my gut, an uneasiness like a tiny tapeworm grew.

The history teacher had given the class an assignment that was due the following week and expected me to hand it in on time even though the other kids had a head start. I scowled but somehow held my tongue. At lunchtime I went to the library to get a World War II book I needed. I half-heartedly searched and finally asked the librarian if she knew where it was. She said it was in the research section, and if it wasn't there, it meant someone was probably using it.

There were a dozen kids in different booths, some working, some sniggering, some canoodling. I pretended to look at books on the shelves while I scanned the tables. I finally spotted my book two booths from the back end of the library. It sat next to the guy who sat next to the book. I cleared my throat.

"Hey are you using this book?" He looked at me and didn't reply. "This book, are you using it?"

He peered at me weird with his werewolfie gray eyes and didn't say anything.

"Don't you remember me?" he said.

"Excuse me?"

"It's only been a couple of months…"

Then he smiled a little, and I remembered. "You're kidding me. Superman?"

"Indeed," he said. He didn't smile. "Do you remember my actual name?"

"Yeah. Donald, right?"

"Actually, it's just Don now."

"Changed your name for political reasons, huh?"

"Something like that." He smirked.

But this guy had changed in more than name. The Donald I remembered had long hair and a crazy unibrow and thick coke-bottle spectacles. His hair was now tight, and his acne had totally cleared up. It was a miraculous transformation.

I understood how puberty worked. I understood that bodies changed over time. But puberty had blasted this guy from weird/ugly to superhot over the summer months. Don was one of the guys who had told me about the Facebook prank Vanessa, Dominique and Bailey had pulled on me earlier that year. He was also part of the Irish dancing flash mob we both took part in.

He stood up and handed me the book, but I didn't take it. I couldn't stop staring.

"You want it or not?" he asked before leaving.

"Oh," I said, blushing, and took it. "You sure you're not using it?"

"I wasn't using it. Besides, I don't need books. It's all in here," he said, poking the side of his head. "See you around." He swung his backpack over his shoulder and left.

I sat dazed and flicked though the book, trying to find the information I needed, but my mind was elsewhere. There was no way I was going to get any work done during lunch, and I sure as hell wasn't coming back to the library after school, so there was only one thing I could do. I carried the book right out of there under my arm.

As we rolled out of school on Friday, a bunch of kids from my grade stood around talking in the parking lot. It was the most delicious temperature, and everyone looked so relaxed sitting by the water fountain. I walked by, slowly noticing Bailey and four or five others laughing.

"What's the move tonight?" I heard Bailey ask.

A small black kid with braces answered. "Wheeler's folks are out of town."

It seemed like everyone was setting up for having fun. I wanted to want to have fun, but I just didn't feel human.

Chapter 27

When I got home, I wanted to dance, knowing it would make me feel better, but could not bring myself to do so. I soon forgot about that when I couldn't find Lucas anywhere and went panicking to Tammy. She told me she had enrolled him in preschool. That was fine until she told me it was called *Hyde and Seek.* I shrieked and grabbed the iPad, mumbling to myself.

"What's the matter?" Tammy asked.

"I'm checking to see how many children have gone missing from that place in the past six months." She looked at me blankly. "Tammy, think about it…The last place you want your kid to go is a place called 'hide and seek'! I mean, we've been through enough. Did you meet the owner? What was she like?

"It was a young man. In a suit."

"Jeez, Tammy," I said, throwing my hands in the air. "You're sending our boy to a preschool called Jekyll and Hyde and Seek? I'm going down there with you tomorrow."

"Why?"

"We're trusting them to look after my brother. I have to beg them not to mess this up. Things are bad enough, you know?"

She couldn't help but smile. I stared open-mouthed at her.

"Alex, I know you've been through a lot lately, but you have to try and relax. The preschool is really excellent, trust me."

Later I calmed down after Lucas told me how much fun it was. He had more friends than me. Despite that I was still feeling super anxious — my breath kept catching, and this unwavering uneasiness kept my shoulders hunched. No matter how often I told myself that this was the beginning of better times, with Grandpa's precarious state, I could not relax.

It wasn't just me who was tense all the time. Tammy had worked nights the previous four days and was exhausted trying to catch up on housework and everything else. Buck was working twelve hours a day Monday to Saturday. Bailey, Kate and I had been helping out, but at dinner time, Tammy tore a sheet of paper from a pad, and we were all assigned daily chores. Even Lucas was included. His job was to bring the recycling to the basement, and he looked so proud to have been given a role. Tammy was due back on day shifts the following week, with a couple of overnights. I would have to collect Lucas from preschool on my way home from school, then help Bailey make dinner. We would take turns going to *Marks* for groceries. On Monday and Tuesday, we chopped and cooked pretty much in silence, but by Wednesday, I decided to make an effort.

"So, I never got to thank you for lending me that money that time Kate and I went to Cincinnati."

Bailey took her headphones out and made me repeat myself.

"Oh yeah, I forgot about that. Thanks for reminding me." She smiled or snarled. "One of these days, I'm gonna come asking for it."

She passed me a bunch of peeled potatoes. I filled a pot with water.

"Actually, you know what, Al? We may be calling in some favors soon enough. I mean we're all hoping and praying you solve your fam problems in Kentucky real soon."

"Why?"

"'Cause we might have to come live with you and this Grandpa guy in Redneckville."

"Huh?"

Bailey paused her tiny music device.

"Haven't you wondered why Mom and Dad are always working?"

"Um, I mean, I guess 'cause they love their jobs?" I asked with a hopeful smile."

"No, you dumbass. It's because of the house. The landlord is selling it, and Mom and Dad have to buy it or else we're homeless. That costs a ton of money."

"Oh," I said.

Bailey went back to her dicing and music, and I stood motionless.

It made sense. Everyone everyplace was struggling to make ends meet. The ideal world of Tammy and Buck I had imagined was also fantasy. The more I thought about it, Lucas and I were lucky to be there at all. It must have been costing them so much extra, not just feeding us but daycare and everything else on top.

Just like that, it was the weekend again. After dinner I took myself and my anxiety into the bedroom once I saw Lucas and Kate had taken control of the TV. I still hadn't started my thousand-word history assignment and was racing against the clock, but when I got down to it, I was too tired and hating everything. Tammy's car pulled up after seven. Bailey screeched and screamed at her. A couple minutes later, Bailey knocked on my door as I doodled in my notebook. Her teeth were clenched, but she was trying her best.

"Alex, some of us are going to Xander's house. He's in your geography class. He's got a karaoke machine or something. You wanna come?"

"No thanks, I gotta do this," I said, tapping at a mostly white sheet of paper.

She seemed relieved. "Ok, suit yourself."

I pinched the bridge of my nose. I hated this, all of it. I pulled out my phone and for no logical reason, looked up pictures of Vinnie on Facebook. There were dozens of pictures of my old class getting ready for Friday night football. I tossed my phone across the floor past Lucas's cot, lay down and closed my eyes.

***

I hardly left the bedroom that weekend. On Sunday evening, Tammy came to find me staring at a blank

Word document. Buck joined her a moment later. My heart started beating fast, thinking something terrible had happened to Grandpa.

"Alex, this won't do. You can't sit here worrying and wasting your life."

I sighed in relief before hanging my head. She sat on the bed beside me. Buck stayed by the door.

"Do you remember when you stole money and sneaked out to ballet classes?"

"Yes." I nodded and perked up. Buck stood with his arms folded, beard doing the talking.

"Well, I almost wish we had that Alex back. Because this version won't do."

"Huh? What do you mean?"

"You need to go on living while you're here, make some friends…and do things." I groaned, and she waited a second before continuing with a little more ferocity. "Kate told me you tried hard to come back for that dancing masterclass, and I could see how jubilant you looked after talking with Kal McGettigan last time. That was something positive in your life, and, well, it's nice to have something positive going on."

Buck cleared his throat before continuing all deep-voiced. "What Tammy is trying to say is your life is pretty shitty." There was a subtle smile somewhere beneath his facial hair. "And when a shitty life offers you something less shitty, you should grab that shit and run with it."

Tammy pursed her lips and rolled her eyes at Buck.

Buck shrugged his shoulder and made a high-pitched noise. "I dunno. Just saying." He turned and walked out.

"Would you like to go to Irish dance classes?"

I shrugged. "What's the point?"

Tammy moved her curled hair this way and that, and her eyes ran all over the place. "Well, there are lots of reasons."

"I was only doing it to humor Kate. The whole thing is crazy."

Tammy rested a warm hand on my leg and stared at me deeply. "It's really not that crazy. Especially if you enjoy it. You've got lots of talent. You remind me of Bailey but obviously not as good."

She said that with a wry smile, and I grimaced at her.

"And Kate. You care about her. She's having a tough time too. Continue for that reason, if no other..."

"I guess." I sulked a second. "Even if I did want to go, the whole thing costs too much money."

"I spoke with Mrs. Gallagher. She said you can join for free provided you help clean up at the end of the night."

I looked at her and felt bad. She was doing her best for all of us. She tried to contain a yawn.

"Ok, I'll give it a go. For like a week. Maybe two."

"Great." She smiled and tapped my leg as she got up.

"One thing though. You'll have to bike. Since Kate's stopped going, I was able to pick up extra shifts at the old folks'."

I nodded. "Roger that."

"You can use Bailey's bike. It shouldn't take any more than thirty minutes."

I nodded. "Ok, I'll give it a try. But I'm not promising anything."

Chapter 28

Kate was due to get the second cast taken off before the end of September, and with her lack of exercise, she had put on weight, and her cheeks were chubbing up. That could have been why she had started snoring at night. Lucas slept without trouble in his little crib, but I was not so fortunate. Not even ear plugs or music would help. Plus, the night train that blasted through Lakewood a couple of times a week was pretty hard to ignore.

One night I couldn't take it anymore. I got up and walked around to calm myself. I wondered if I cleaned up the basement, I could set up shop down there — maybe fix up a little bed. As I crept down the groaning stairs, I heard the faint sound of an electric guitar. There he was, old Buckster, sitting on a wooden chair, a metal-blue guitar strapped around his big frame. He was riffing something bluesy.

"Did I know this about you, old man?"

His left hand continued to slide up and down the frets, his other gently picking the strings. I looked 'round. The place was totally reorganized. The washer and dryer were shoved into a corner to make space for a drum kit and mic stand. There was a keyboard and a laptop and wires and all sorts of electronic equipment.

"Me and my buddy, we jam here every now and then. Just for fun."

I didn't quite believe it was just for fun, not with the soundboard and music mixers.

"What you doing down here?" he asked.

"Aw, I don't mean to be rude, mister, but Kate won't stop snoring."

"You can't sleep down here. This is my bat-cave. In fact, you shouldn't be here. Leave!" he said, and started riffing some more.

I opened my mouth to speak, but he stopped playing and interrupted my efforts.

"Alex. Go upstairs. I'm having Buck time."

I went back into the bedroom, but Kate kept snoring. I nudged her gently, but nothing happened. I gritted my teeth, knowing how horrible a person I was being. I held her nose until she started coughing and choking, and she turned onto her side. It worked. The snoring stopped. I lay down and tried to relax in the silence but still couldn't sleep. I felt so bad about what I'd just done to Kate. Thankfully, the next morning, she had no idea of the incident.

"Alex, I had this dream last night," she said at breakfast the following morning as she spooned ice cream into a bowl.

"You managed to dream through all that snoring?" I joked. She licked her spoon, her plump little face grinning. I contemplated scolding her for eating junk for breakfast but stopped myself. That was something Debby might do. I hated my DNA. I had to make a conscious effort not to be like her.

"I had this dream we were all at a feis together, and we all came home with trophies. And it was the bestest dream I had in days."

"That sounds cool."

"I almost had another bestest dream after it."

"What was that?"

"I dreamt I had a time machine and I went back in time and found a dinosaur egg and brought it to the future and it grew out of its egg."

"Hatched?"

"Yeah, it did, and I trained it to be my secret weapon."

"Nice! Then what?"

"Well, everything was going according to plan until we nearly conquered the government, but then he fell in love with a female dinosaur."

"Where did that come from?"

"Don't even ask," she said, waving away my question in annoyance. "So then when the government killed his girlfriend, he got really angry and…"

Kate trailed off.

"And what?"

"And he ate me."

"Aw, that's too bad. Better luck next time, I guess?"

Feeling bad for her, I decided it was time to do as Tammy said, even though I wasn't in the mood.

"I was thinking of doing a little dancing today. You want to come and help?"

She nodded excitedly, then scampered off on her crutches and came back with her iPad.

"What's that for?"

"I'm going to record you dancing, and then I can show you where you need to improve. Dream, believe, achieve, Alex."

I grimaced. Motivational clichés were the worst.

Kate did her best to teach me, but it was hard for her on so many levels. She had me working on my hornpipe and kept yelling at me to turn out my feet and making sure I was getting all my beats.

As the session went on, Kate's demeanor changed. Sometimes she would grit her teeth and smack her fingers on the cast of her leg. Later I found her in the basement, her eyes all puffy. She said there was nothing the matter, but I knew that it was hard for her to watch me dance when there was a real chance she might never dance again. It was heartbreaking. But I felt a whole lot better after the exercise. It was mood medicine.

Every night before bedtime, I watched an episode of *Reel Rebels* on YouTube and wondered what Kal McGettigan was up to and if I'd ever bump into him again. Fuzz texted me to see how everything was going. I told him I was about to join a dance class, and he told me to keep up the good work.

Chapter 29

The following Thursday night, I got the greatest surprise when I went on Facebook and saw a friend request from Michelle. She happened to be online, so we started chatting. She wanted to know when I'd be coming back. She was madly in love with her new boyfriend, and her profile was filled with disgusting loved-up pictures of the two of them. That made me sick, and I told her so, but she didn't care. That's what happiness was—not giving a damn when people were negative toward you.

After shutting the lid on my laptop, I thought hard about my friend situation. I was happy in my own company but only to an extent. I didn't have anyone to hang out with in Lakewood. The most stimulating conversations I had were with Kate and Lucas and sometimes Tammy. I tried to comfort myself by saying it was temporary.

But after school on Friday, a bunch of Bailey's friends gathered in the parking lot, asking in hushed voices, "What's the move tonight?" Nobody thought to include me. I gritted my teeth and kept walking. It didn't matter. There was no point. There was no point in making an effort with kids I didn't even care about who weren't even going to be in my life a couple months later. It was just a matter of time before Lucas and I found ourselves on a bus back to Kentucky.

And besides — *The Move*? Big whoop! Sometimes *The Move* was nothing more than hanging at the pizza place on Maddison. Everybody was secretly looking for a party where they could get trashed drunk, but I wasn't so sure that happened much. I had yet to see Bailey come home late, stumbling all over the place.

On Saturday after sleeping in, I woke so bored I wanted to eat my hair. With Kate entertaining Lucas, I felt fine leaving him behind and taking a stroll to the coffee shop to see if Nellie was working. The shop front had changed and was now a fluorescent lilac, with *Novo* in yellow letters. The interior had been stripped back, with a wooden bench theme going on, and they had inserted a waterfall feature in the center of the room. Down back was still old school, like a library, except the shelves were rugged wood and not the Ikea kind. I was pleased to see the collection of vinyls and DJ booth remained.

Nellie spotted me right away as I looked around the place and ran over with a loud 'hey' and hugged me. I was kinda taken aback because she had completely changed her hair — no more black bangs. It was short, spiky and purple-red. Her lip was pierced, and she had a tattoo of a dove on her wrist. She told her boss she was taking fifteen, and we sat down.

"How long you staying for this time?"

"It's only temporary." I grimaced. "How are you doing?"

"Good. I'm getting a degree in fine arts and you know, just basically trying to save up some money. I really wanna do a semester in Paris."

"That sounds cool."

"Cleveland State is a pretty good school. You should consider it in a few years' time."

"Um, yeah, it sounds great, except I have to think about Lucas and Kentucky."

"Oh yeah, of course," said Nellie with brief sadness, but she quickly perked up. "Oh hey, how about next Sunday we go on a picnic to Lakewood Park?"

"Yeah, that could be good."

"What else are you getting up to?"

I blushed. "I'm kinda doing a little Irish dancing. I start classes next week."

"Wow, shut up! That's awesome!"

"It is?" I asked, surprised.

"Duh! Me and my Mom went to see *Passion of the Dance* downtown like five years ago. It was so good."

There was a little pause, then her eyes lit up. "Now, tell me about boys. See anything you like?"

I rolled my eyes. "Well, there is one guy who is kinda cute. Actually, he used to Irish dance too. But there's no point," I said, snarling.

"Why?"

"It's just, it's my mom. And my dad. Things are tough, you know?"

I briefly told her everything that had been going on. Nellie listened with big eyes but didn't stir except for crossing one leg over the other.

"I guess all you can do is hope things work out with your grandpa. But man, what a bummer not being able to stay here for longer."

I frowned. "There's no point in making friends here. This kid, Don. What's the point, right? There's no point dating," I said, all loud and frank. Nellie looked at me like a kitten who had just been abandoned.

"All you can do, Alex girl, is try and have the time of your life while you're here. Make the most of it. Treat it like a vacation. Forget about school. Forget studying. Have fun. Do stuff. Dance and hang out. Make plenty of moves. You can't do anything about the other stuff, so try and park it. Go dance with that kid." She started rolling her shoulders in this disgusting erotic way. "Dancey, dancey, dancey."

I laughed. "You're disgusting. But I guess you're right."

We had to say goodbye when Nellie's manager came over. He was a young guy with a shaved head and a little beard coming out of his chin that had been braided. "Ellen, it's been fifteen minutes times three."

"Whatever, Jarrod."

She scratched her number on a piece of paper from the register and handed it to me. "See you soon, Alex girl."

As I walked home, I thought about everything she'd said. Nellie was right. I'd have to try and put the misery to the back of my mind and have some fun.

Chapter 30

On Sunday night, I saw pics of Vinnie and Kimberly on Facebook, cuddling and posing, and I almost allowed myself to get angry but quickly remembered what Nellie had said. That stuff didn't matter. The following day at school, I took action. I asked a girl called Kelli if Don was dating anyone, and she laughed. She said, "The artist formerly known as Donald might be the new hot stuff, but his personality is so not." She finished with a braced smile.

At lunch time, I walked around looking to accidentally-on-purpose bump into Don. I finally found him around the football stands, where kids usually went to smoke. He was sitting on his lonesome, texting.

"You quit smoking?" I asked.

He nodded. "Once I read up on what really happens—the nicotine trap and all—I was like, I'm done. Those guys don't give a crap about people. We are just consumer slaves." He shook his head, angry.

"So listen, I kinda need your help."

"My help?"

"Yeah. My cousin Kate. She wants me to take up Irish dancing full time."

He sniggered. "Where did this come from?"

"I'm humoring her. You know she broke her leg real bad. She might never dance again."

"Ouch," he said, clenching his teeth. A couple of seconds of silence went by as he drew a shape with his foot in some stone chips. His body warmed and softened as he turned toward me. "That's nice of you to do that…To try and cheer her up."

"So I'm joining class next week, but I was hoping to do some practice in the garage before, you know? But when I asked Kate to come watch, it made her so sad." I let him wallow in that misery for a bit, then went a different route. "You're a pretty advanced dancer, right? You think you could maybe come 'round some day and check on how I'm doing?"

He looked away and shrugged. Finally, he answered. "I mean, I guess. I guess I've got an hour tomorrow. After five."

"Great." I pulled his cell phone from his hand and punched in my number. Don blushed and started to fidget. Had he been wearing glasses, they would have fogged up.

"My house tomorrow at five." I swung my head 'round and strutted away. I was feeling victorious.

***

Surprisingly, the next day, I was like a nervous Purvis waiting for Don to come. I must have changed practice clothes five times and fixed my hair a dozen times. We both ended up blushing real hard when I opened the door to let him in. We were dressed identically in white tanks and black shorts. And if that wasn't bad enough, Bailey passed through to the living room and caught a glance.

"You get freakier by the day, Al." She stopped with her cup of tea and stared at the two of us. "Are they your little sister's shorts, Don?" she asked with a smirk. I grabbed his arm and rushed him outside, heading for the garage.

"Nice dance space you got here," he said as he rallied on the layers of wood floor and glanced at the mounted stereo and mirrors. "Is there anything in particular you want help with?"

"Um, I'm not sure. How about I dance through all my light shoe dances, and you take a look?"

I played some music and went through all the dances one by one. Don didn't say anything, just watched with an impressed smirk.

"You're doing pretty well for a beginner," he said blankly.

"Thank you!"

"I have an idea. I think you'll like this. There's this move called a bicycle. We can put it in your reel, and it will make it look lots better." Don demonstrated. It involved kicking my butt with both feet a bunch of times before landing.

Don danced the steps alongside me. His calves were as big as my thighs. He was actually quite a nice dancer. I just wondered if whatever weight exercises he was doing made it hard for him to stand straight when he danced.

We worked on it for thirty minutes solid. It was pretty tough, but soon I started getting the hang of it. After a while, Kate came into the garage and sat quietly in the corner on a high stool. I could tell she was a little sore. She wanted to be involved in anything I was up to. Everything was fine for the first while, but soon a shitstorm hit. Kate was blowing and puffing as she watched me dance.

"You're dropping your heel on the hop back," said Kate. "Don, show her how to do it right."

I stepped aside, and Don did the move.

"Don!" Kate snapped. "That ain't right either."

"Yes, it is," he argued.

"Nuh-uh. Look in the mirror. Go on, try again."

Don danced it again. Kate was right, he was adding in an extra beat.

"See, you did it again," wailed Kate.

"What are you talking about? It's perfect."

"Are you blind or something?" Kate responded. I bit my lip, trying not to laugh. Don's fuse was borderline explosive. He was a sexy, sweaty mess. He spoke calmly, sarcasm to the rescue.

"Actually, Kate, I have an astigmatism of the left eye. So I hope you're happy!" He smiled smartly at her.

"Whatever. I'm going to get a drink." Kate hobbled off on her crutches. Don's face finally broke into a grin.

At the end, my hamstrings were starting to cramp, so Don helped me stretch them out. For such a serious guy, I could tell he had a softer side. As he got ready to leave, he said, "I hope I was of some help. I guess if you need more advice, you can text me. But *only* if it's an emergency. 'cause I hate to say it, Alex, it's me or the devil-child."

We both grinned. I'd known Kate had a little temper, but this was another level.

Don said goodbye. I had a funny feeling in my gut as I watched him walk off.

After dinner I relaxed by the TV. Kate and her crutches entered. She picked up the remote control, which was by my side, and turned off the TV. Then her fiery eyes pierced mine.

"Please don't ask alien-face to come to our house anymore," she said, flicking her head to the right, meaning Don. "He won't teach you much either." A puzzled look came over her face. "You need to join Mrs. Gallagher's class, because the truth is, I can't teach you, and bird brain can't neither. You know that Mr. Fuzz in Kentucky? He doesn't even have a school. If you go back to Kentucky, you can't go to feiseanna or nothing. Least here you can do those things."

Even though my brain told me not to, I laughed right in her face.

"I'm serious, Alex," she said firmly.

"Ok, ok," I said apologetically, giggling.

Kate might have been right about Don's potential as a dance teacher. But he had other potentials. That night before bed, I mulled it over for a while before cracking, and I texted him.

Tomorrow at five. It's an emergency.

Then I turned my phone off and refused to check until morning.

Chapter 31

Don couldn't come the next day, but it didn't matter, because Thursday I gathered the courage to go to dance class. I was sweating so much from the bike ride, which took almost forty minutes. Mrs. Gallagher was talking with some moms as I entered, and I felt so awkward, not knowing where to go or what to do. There were ten little ones, including Martin, who I had met before, doing drills. Lucy spotted me and came skipping over with a smile. Lucy was Mrs. Gallagher's best dancer and a year older than me. We had met the previous winter and danced in a flash mob together.

"Hey, you decided to join?" I nodded shyly. "That's cool. I guess you got inspired by Kal McGettigan's class? I saw you there."

"Yeah," I said, nodding enthusiastically. "He's amazing."

Lucy snorted when she laughed. "Oh boy, I know. Try spending a week in his company." Lucy had long, fair hair and a sharpish nose, but she was cute in her own way.

"Oh wow, you went to the week-long? How was it?"

"It was good but really tough. He tried out some new choreography with us. It was modern dance mingled with Irish, so kinda weird and hard to get right."

"Is it true he was looking for dancers for his new show?"

Lucy took a drink from her water bottle and shrugged. "Honestly, no one knows. I mean, some of the older girls kept asking him, but all he said was that he was keeping his eyes open for interesting dancers. He did say that something big was on the horizon, though, and we'd know more before Oireachtas."

"Big?"

Just as I wanted to probe further, Mrs. Gallagher's big frame made its way towards us. She was wearing a long green St. Patrick's Day t-shirt with a white shamrock on the back.

"Lucy dear, glad to see you're looking after our newest member. Do you mind runnin' Alex through the dances she's gonna need?"

"Sure," said Lucy. Mrs. Gallagher trundled off.

"Ok, how old are you? When was your birthday?"

"Um, I turned fifteen in February," I said, noticing that I stood a couple inches taller than her.

"Ok, so you'll be dancing U Fifteen." She said 'U' instead of under. "K, what have you got so far?"

"Um, I guess I'm a Beginner Two in everything."

"What's your set?"

I shook my head. "Nope, no set just yet."

We both laughed at the rhyming words.

"Ok, I'll teach you a basic one. It's called *The Storyteller*."

She taught me the dance, which was really short and pretty easy. After fifteen minutes, she went to work on her own steps, and I worked alone. Mrs. Gallagher had the little ones going up and down the hall in lines. Lucy came back to me towards the end of class, and I showed her how I had done.

"Nice, Alex, you learn fast," said Lucy. "I cannot get over how good you are for a beginner."

I smiled. I really appreciated her giving up her time for me.

"You seem ready to start competing."

"You think?"

She nodded strongly.

"I guess. I mean I don't know how long I'm going to be in Cleveland."

"Well, there are feiseanna every weekend. Some small ones, then some bigger ones. There won't be too many beginner dancers for you to compete against, so it won't be hard for you to move up the ladder."

I was starting to feel really good about myself. Lucy had a way of talking that would put anyone at ease. She explained how the steps would become increasingly difficult as I progressed.

"I recommend setting goals. That's what I do. Everything I do now will be prep for the next major, which is Oireachtas, at the end of November."

"Cool. Where do you hope to place?"

"Hmm, well, I placed top twenty last year, so top fifteen would be awesome, I guess."

"Wow, this business requires serious effort, huh."

Lucy nodded. "Oh yeah. It sure puts the dead in dedication."

At the end of class, I stacked up the chairs and swept and mopped the floor. It didn't take much more than twenty-five minutes. After that, I thanked Mrs. Gallagher and cycled home before showering and slouching exhausted onto the couch.

***

Later that evening, Tammy asked me to call Grandpa. She had received a text from Peggy earlier saying he was getting stronger and wanted to hear our voices.

"You received a text message? That old bat can text?" I asked in a surprised tone. But Tammy didn't see the funny side.

"Your sick old grandpa misses you, and that's what you want to focus on? Peggy's technological ability? Go get Lucas and make the call."

Peggy answered the phone, and I waited for almost two minutes before Grandpa made it to the receiver. His voice rasped a little.

"How are you, Gramps?"

"Oh, fine. I'm not done on this earth just yet. You kids behaving up at the lake?"

"We are. Lucas is doing real good. We both miss you, though."

"I'm getting stronger every day, and Peggy's taking good care of me. Those people from Child Protection came 'round. They found out your father's working full time at Fort Knox, but he's not too keen on coming back to Alderhill just yet."

That news kind of hit me for six, and all of a sudden, I felt queasy. Tammy was hovering around me, all anxious. She mouthed some words at me, and in a daze, I said goodbye to Grandpa and handed her the phone.

After a while, Tammy brought me a cup of tea.

"You feel better after hearing Grandpa's voice?"

"I guess," I said, unsure.

"He said your mom is living with Dorothy and has been getting counselling. I'm going to have to take a run down there…Grandpa is going to give Buck and I some money to help get this mortgage."

Tammy looked so pale when she said that, and I didn't understand why. I wondered what it meant if Grandpa was giving money to Tammy and Buck to help buy the house. Did that make it more likely that Lucas and I could stay longer in Lakewood? On the flip side, the fact that he was getting better probably meant it was only a matter of time before we went back to live with him. I hated how unsettling the whole thing was, especially now that I had goals and dreams I wanted to achieve. Was it worth making the effort if it was all for nothing? I figured I at least had to try.

Sean de Gallai

Chapter 32

Motivated by Lucy's words, I practiced for hours and hours at home every day after school. I felt like asking Don over at the weekend but decided against it. I couldn't go to dance class on Tuesday night because Tammy and Buck were both working and Bailey went out, so I had to keep an eye on Kate and Lucas. For some reason, I was full of energy and decided to give bored-stiff Kate a chance to get involved in my dancing once more and hoped it wouldn't make her sad.

Kate smiled graciously as I danced.

"Alex, this stuff is real good, real tight. You need to ask Mrs. Gallagher to teach you harder steps."

I nodded. "You know, Lucy said she always sets herself targets to achieve by certain dates. You think I should set some?"

"Set targets, prepare, plan, work, achieve."

"Okaayyyy....?"

"Targets are vital, Alex. Duh! Everyone knows that."

"Well, last time I remember you set me a target of becoming World Champion, but that's not exactly realistic, now is it?"

"I guess not."

"So what is realistic, Kate? Come on, kid, work with me here."

"Hmm, maybe you could be a prizewinner by Christmas? I think you're good enough to get out of beginner and Novice soon, but I guess it all depends how you do when the steps get harder. You need to go to a feis real soon."

At Thursday's class, I spent the first twenty minutes dancing on my own, then Mrs. Gallagher came over. She asked me to work on all my other beginner dances and watched for less than ten minutes, not saying anything other than 'good, keep going'. As I cleaned up the hall, she spoke to me once more.

"There's a feis on Sunday. I think it would be nice if you came with the class."

"Sure." I nodded enthusiastically.

"Good girl. It might be fun. There's no need to worry. Nobody's expecting anything. Kate will help you get organized. She'll enjoy that."

She was right about that. On Saturday night, Kate made me hand wash my skirt and leotard and polish my shoes. We laid everything out nice and neat on my bed before folding it away into one of Kate's old dance bags. My hair was almost down to my neck, and because I didn't have a wig, I was going to pin it out of my eyes. Kate left a bottle of spray tan on my bedside locker and told me to make sure it had dried before I got in bed. But by that stage, I was too tired to apply it and figured I'd do so in the morning or not at all—after all, I hadn't used any at the Arlington feis so figured there was probably no need.

Tammy was more than happy to bring Kate and me early the following morning.

The feis was in a school gym in a town called Parma, which was just over thirty minutes' drive away. Mrs. Gallagher's class all had matching shorts, jackets and dress bags with a pink and black GSD design — Gallagher's School of Dance. She gathered her team of eighteen or so littles age four to twelve and gave them their instructions. Lucy knew the drill and did her own thing. I was glad Tammy and Kate were there to help me, because Mrs. Gallagher had plenty of work organizing the littler ones. She even had a hard time getting Martin on track, as he wanted to hang out and talk to Kate.

I changed into my black skirt and leotard, and Tammy pinned back my hair. I warmed up outside and stretched before coming back into the practice area and running through all my light shoe dances. My competition was starting at ten. Mrs. Gallagher came over, looking a little flustered.

"Alex, your legs are all white."

"Why thank you, Mrs. Gallagher." I smiled and winked at Kate. But Kate clasped both hands over her mouth.

"No, I'm serious. Your legs are all pasty and white."

"Oh, I thought you momentarily had problems with your R's."

"I told you last night, Alex," said Kate.

"Why didn't you put tan on?" Mrs. Gallagher asked.

"Um, I didn't think it was necessary?"

"Oh darling, you can't go out dancing like this. It looks unprofessional. Did you bring a pair of dark tights?"

I swallowed hard and whispered no. Tammy looked at Mrs. Gallagher and then at me and with pursed lips, unzipped her handbag and dangled her keys.

"Target. I'll scoot over to Target."

Up until that point, I had felt fine. It was just a fun day out, keeping everyone happy and ticking along. But all of a sudden, it felt like Armageddon. The announcers then called all the Beginner Two dancers side stage. Then I began to panic. I was going to get disqualified at my first feis for Mrs. Gallagher. It wasn't so much the embarrassment of getting disqualified that concerned me as the fact that I had parted with sixty hard-earned bucks for the entrance fee and all for nothing. That money would have been better spent on ice cream.

I had to think fast. Mrs. Gallagher shook her head with displeasure as I ran up to the announcer and pleaded with her to wait two minutes, rubbing my knees together to show her just how badly I needed the bathroom. Luckily, Tammy came running through a crowd of people and handed me a pair of tights.

"Quick, put them on."

"Here?" I asked, looking 'round.

"Yes!" Tammy nodded quickly. The other two Under Fifteen girls walked onto the stage. Tammy tore the wrapping off the tights, and I quickly pulled them on and ran over to join the other girls.

Flustered, just as the music started, I noticed my lace had come a little undone, so I bent over quick to tuck it into my soft shoe and felt a whole bunch of cool air and sweat escape where the tights had ripped — right from my butt to the back of my knee on the left leg. I started dancing anyway, trying to catch up, as graceful as a human possibly could be with their backside on show, my face bright red with shame. I spotted Mrs. Gallagher shaking her head and walking away before I had even finished.

We stayed on stage and went through all the light shoe dances, and I really just wanted the day to end.

I came off stage, found a seat, threw a towel over my head and placed it between my knees.

"Oh gosh, Alex, too bad about the tights. But the dancing was nice," said Kate.

I flung the towel across the floor and glared at Tammy. "Can we go now? Please."

But Tammy's face was serious.

"Alex, you won't often hear me say this. You want to give up because your tights ripped?"

"Yes, Tammy," I whined.

"Four words." She gave each word equal attention. "Who. Gives. A. Crap? You're going to need that skin to start toughening up quick. This is a good place to start. Your dancing was nice."

Kate arrived back. "The heavy shoe dances are right after the Under Eights. There are like nine girls in that comp."

Tammy made this dumb face at me. "There you go. What have you learned? The heavy jig?"

I shook my head. "The hornpipe."

"The hornpipe. Go practice in the hall. With Kate. Now." She ushered me away with her eyebrows.

First thing I did was tear off the tights and throw them in the trash. I found it pretty hard to give a damn when I was practicing with Kate, but she wouldn't have any of it.

"Alex do you even know what PMA means?" She didn't wait for me to answer. "Positive mental attitude. You are being way too negative right now."

"Katie, I was terrible."

"You are wrong. Come here." She got her phone out of her pocket and began to scroll. "Look."

She had recorded my dancing and played it back to me. Kate was right. I had danced pretty neatly, every single dance. The only thing not so nice was the repulsive face on my face.

"Maybe try smiling next time, huh?" said Kate.

I also realized how poor my competitors were. After that, I felt more positive. Kate ran me through the hornpipe several times with almost zero corrections, and soon I was back on stage with the others to dance the hornpipe. They wrapped up the Under Fifteen Beginner Two results almost immediately afterward.

I came first in every single dance. Mrs. Gallagher just said, "Good start, Alex. See you Tuesday."

We got in the car, and Tammy had this mischievous expression. She looked across at me and smacked my leg and smiled. It was something Buck would do.

"Jeez, Alex, that was great. Your first feis, and you swept up."

"Yeah, I guess."

"I guess? You're into Novice. We need to get ice cream."

I hadn't seen Tammy this happy in so long. She had body-swapped with Kate as we went to *Honey Hut* for ice cream.

"Boy, that Mrs. Gallagher sure can be a party pooper. 'Well done' was all she could think of. You're a gorgeous dancer, Alex."

"See, I told you, Mom," said Kate, slurping a cone.

"I have some advice for you. You're doing real well keeping your body straight, and you look pretty when you dance, but why don't you try and attack the stage next time?"

I squinted at her. "Attack? The stage?" and I allowed a second to pass before continuing to mock Tammy. "You want me to attack the stage? Good one, Tam. Yeah, I'll be sure to do that." Then I broke out laughing, and Kate followed suit, the laughter contagious.

"You know what? Forget about it," said Tammy in annoyance. "That's the last advice you'll get from me. You know, you are such a brat sometimes." She focused on the driving, her mouth taut, but I just giggled and tapped her leg.

I was feeling so warm and happy with myself. This was how things were supposed to be.

Chapter 33

The following Tuesday, Tammy drove me to Rocky River for dance class because she wanted to talk to Mrs. G. about Kate. As I got warmed up, I kept an eye on their conversation. Tammy did most of the talking, looking quite stern, and eventually, Mrs. Gallagher began nodding in agreement. After Tammy left, Mrs. Gallagher came over.

"I need you working much harder now. I've got new steps for you to learn. Lucy?" she yelled. "Come on over here." Lucy, who was helping a couple of girls, obeyed.

"Lucy, we're going to focus on Alex's reel, hornpipe and set now. Ok?"

Lucy spent the next two classes preparing me for Novice dances. The hornpipe music slowed down, yet the steps became faster and more complicated. It was hard for me to get my head around them at first. The reel became harder and was now forty-eight bars. We decided not to go to the following weekend's feis so that I could work on the new steps and save money for when I was ready to compete at a later date. It was almost sixty bucks or more at a time.

That meant I had a couple of free weekends. I could sense Don was keen to hang out with me a little more, but weekends were the only spare time we both had, especially with Don studying for the SATs. I was so happy when he finally plucked up the courage to ask me out on a proper date.

Math had just finished, and I was making my way to biology when Don came up behind me and tapped me on the shoulder. I kept walking, and he followed.

"Hey, I just wanted to say I know you probably started dance classes, but if you ever need some further expertise, well, I'm available."

I waited for him to laugh, but Don genuinely thought he was being cool. I cringed and wondered if I was right to hope for what was coming.

"Thanks, Don. I'll let you know, ok?"

"Great. I mean good."

I kept walking, and he stood in shock for a moment before reevaluating his confidence, then followed after like a scared puppy. I closed my eyes briefly and pressed my lips together; I could feel his next move coming. He had to do it quick before I got to my classroom.

"So, you know I play in a band."

"Oh?" I said, lyrical.

"Well, actually, it's a one-man band."

I gave him my eyebrowed 'that's weird' face. He bit his bottom lip and inhaled. "Yeah, so there's this battle of the bands competition at Floyd's Coffee Shop on Detroit. Do you want to come?"

"Battle of the Bands sounds fun. Josh has a band," I remembered loudly.

"The Wild Slices." Don nodded. "Those guys will be there too, except their music sucks." There was a long, awkward pause, and I wondered if he could follow through. Finally, the words came bumbling out.

"So, I guess… If you aren't doing anything, maybe you wanna come? I mean, you don't have to."

"Sure," I said. "When?"

His eyes almost popped out of his skull.

"Wow. I mean. Good. Great."

"When's it happening?"

"Yes. It's happening. I mean Saturday. At Floyd's. On Detroit."

"OK. Saturday when?"

"Oh, of course. I mean, at eight."

"Ok, that should be fine."

He blushed and waved at me as I stood in front of him. "Ok, great. I'll text you. So long." Then he turned and hustled on out of there.

"So long?" I whispered to myself, and made a sour face. Did I really want to date a guy who said farewells from the 1850's?

But I was actually very excited. Excited that I had something to do with one of the hottest guys in town, and it was kinda cute how he was folding like the worst card player ever right in front of my eyes. It was nice to feel sought after.

On Saturday night, for the first time in years, I dressed up in something other than jeans and a shirt. Earlier that day, I'd gone to the thrift store and found a cute black knee-length dress with a crimson flower print and wore it with my gray zip-up hoodie and converse, figuring it was sufficiently cool for live music. The best part was, it only cost four dollars.

Don picked me up at six-thirty. I kept asking him what kind of music he played, but he just said it was a surprise. His mom had dropped his guitar at Floyd's earlier that day.

We got there kinda early so that he could set up his slot, but soon the place was packed with kids, teachers and parents. Don pointed out a reporter and photographer from a Lakewood newspaper. The coffee shop served mocktails. I had strawberry daiquiris until I could no longer stand the brain freeze.

There were eight different acts, and without question, Josh's band was the most proficient. I actually got goosebumps when it was Don's turn, having no idea what to expect.

To say I was surprised was an understatement. Don's handsome jaw line and lean, muscly figure did not make up for his lack of talent. He played his guitar and rapped! It was miserable and rhythmless, and the lyrics were terrible. But he thought he was God's gift to the music industry and pulled pained expressions as he played, trying to emit emotion while flexing his biceps and chest muscles through his tight, white tee. I cringed hard, but all the other girls stared with twinkling eyes.

Afterwards he walked me home. He was on cloud nine after performing, and I had a terrible feeling his overconfidence would lead to him trying to kiss me. I cut him off at the pass.

"Well done, champ. I had fun. Thanks for a nice night," I said sharply, and kissed him on the cheek before running inside. When I got inside, I looked out the window and saw him standing where I'd left him, touching his cheek where I had kissed it.

I shook my head and grinned. He was pathetic putty. But he was my putty.

Chapter 34

A couple of things happened all at once on the fifteenth of September. Kate got called to the hospital to have her cast removed. The doctors were extremely pleased with how her leg had healed. She was going to make a full recovery, and her mood blasted to new levels of hyperactivity. She had to wear a 'space boot' for a further month, but after that, she could start rehabilitation.

After talking on the phone to Grandpa, Tammy came to speak with me.

"I'm going to take a run to Alderhill to visit Dad. I was wondering if you'd like to come?"

"When?"

"This weekend."

I exhaled. "I mean, I'd like to, but…I don't really want to."

"Huh?" said Tammy.

"I have things this weekend. It's my first feis as a Novice, and I kinda wanted to hang out with some friends…If you go Monday, I'll come."

Tammy shook her head. "It has to be this weekend. Your grandpa is giving Buck and I some money to help make up the down payment…It can't wait."

I nodded. When I thought about what Tammy was actually doing—asking a sick, old man for money—I realized how awful that must have been for her. I felt sad when I thought about Grandpa and wanted to see him, but at the back of my mind, I remembered how short my time in Lakewood would be. Lucas and I would be back in Kentucky soon enough for long enough. Attendance at all the dance classes and feiseanna was vital. I had to keep improving while I had the help of Mrs. Gallagher and the ease of access to competitions in Cleveland.

On Friday Tammy took off for Alderhill and arranged with Lucy's Mom to bring me to the feis that Saturday. It was held in a suburb of Cleveland called Troy. Lucy texted me at seven-thirty on Saturday morning to let me know they were on their way. I sat into Lucy's mom's old beige Nissan and did a double take — they could have been sisters. The only difference was Lucy's mom's hair was dark, dark black.

"Nice to meet you, Alex, I'm Joan. You all excited for your big day?"

Lucy turned 'round. "I told Mom it was your first in Novice."

"I am excited. I missed the last couple of feiseanna to practice. For some reason, Mrs. Gallagher thinks I'll come first in all the dances, but I'm not so sure."

Joan laughed. "Oh, she's probably right. You'll see."

True to her word, as I registered, I got the funniest look from the lady at the table.

"Ms. Maslow, you'll be competing all your dances one after another, I think."

I had half-expected that, but the lady wasn't finished.

"Seems like you're the only girl competing Under Fifteen Novice today." She smiled.

It was actually quite weird. After I got warmed up and ran through my dances, an organizer came and asked me to come to one of the side stages in the gym. Mrs. Gallagher came shuffling along and actually told the musician to wait while she grabbed a piece of paper and a pen from the organizer. Then she nodded, and the musician started playing. I danced my reel, and straight after I had finished, Mrs. Gallagher stood waiting for me side stage with my heavy shoes.

"Go on, dear. They are waiting to get you all done."

I quickly tied up my heavies, and they didn't even give me time to practice. I danced my hornpipe as best as I could with the quicker steps and slower music, and after I bowed, the music for *The Storyteller* set started up straight away. I had no option but to stay where I was and dance it through.

I walked off stage to Joan clapping, which was kind of embarrassing. She handed me my water bottle. Mrs. Gallagher was talking with a young male judge and scribbling on her paper. Eventually, she came over to me and shoved her sweaty hand into mine and shook it strongly.

"Oh my, well done, Alex. I knew you would come first, but it's the manner in which you have won—the judge scored you very highly." She quickly uncorked the lid of a water bottle and took little sips before continuing. Her eyes beamed. "I've never had anyone start dancing so late in life and become very good. Most girls start as babies and dance for hours and hours and years and years, and most still don't get very good."

I nodded. It reminded me of a quote by Malcolm Gladwell. He said it took ten thousand hours of practice to reach genius level of anything. How many had I danced? Not even five hundred? I had a long way to go.

The announcer came over with a bunch of medals. "Well done. You danced very nicely. Here you go, first place." She grinned.

Mrs. Gallagher said 'thank you' and turned back to me.

"Tammy's grandma must have been some kind of thoroughbred, because you and Kate have so much natural ability. And let's not forget Bailey, who was my first Nans Champion as an Under Twelve."

I had forgotten about Bailey. I reminded myself to ask her later why she had given up if she was so good.

"I just love your upper body technique and your presentation. Your elevation and timing...Really, you've got a lot going for you."

"Thanks, Mrs. Gallagher."

"You'll be dancing in Prizewinner now. There'll be a lot more girls competing for first place, but I'm excited to see how you do. We should skip a couple of feiseanna and work on your steps, and if, and this is a big if," she paused for effect. "If you do well over the next few weeks, I'll consider bringing you to Oireachtas."

"Really?" I yelped. "Great, Mrs. Gallagher. Thank you so much."

I had not been expecting that. It felt awesome to be complimented like that. I now had a shot of going to my first and only ever major dance competition. It was so exciting.

***

I texted Fuzz when I got home, and he called me straight away.

"That's amazing, Alex, but remember what I told you about patience. Get all the experience you can up there, 'cause it's going to be much harder when you come back. Keep me posted. Bye."

When I told Kate, her hyperactivity was infectious, and I let the fantasy drive my mood. She could not stop talking about it at dinner.

"This is so exciting. I remember when I qualified out of Novice. But it was different. You had to beat zero other people, but there were thirty-three girls in my comp."

"Turty-tree and a turd," said Bailey in a dumb Irish accent, momentarily interrupting. Kate stuck out her tongue.

"Is this meant to be a compliment, Kate?" Buck asked. "It started out like one, but now it's like you're saying Alex won 'cause she was the only girl there?"

"Be quiet, Dad. What I meant was, I remember how exciting it was to progress up the chain." Kate's eyes were all big and white and serious.

"Either way, Alex, now you'll need to get a job."

Buck banged the table real hard and smiled. Some milk spilled out of Lucas's cup. He looked scared for a millisecond.

"Finally, Kate says the most intelligent thing this century. Get a job. Y'all get out of my house and get a job. You too, Kate, go on now," he said in his best Kentucky accent.

"Be quiet, Dad," said Kate.

"Why do I need a job?"

"'Cause you need a dress, dummy!"

"What's wrong with my black'n'black?"

"It's Oireachtas, Alex. You gotta make an impression. You're gonna need a wig too."

I shook my head in her face. "No way. I like my hair short. And I AM making an impression. I won't look like every other girl there. How is that not making an impression?"

She looked at me blankly.

Kate probably had a point about getting a job. Even if I didn't want to buy a dress or wig, it was still a major expense to enter Oireachtas and get to Chicago, with hotels and whatnot.

Kate continued. "You know, most families save up all their money to go to majors. Like Martin's family? His mom saves up all their money so they can enter and dance, and when they go someplace, they stay and do sightseeing and stuff and make it like their summer vacation, except sometimes it's in the fall. These things can cost like a thousand dollars."

I thought she was exaggerating but stopped chewing when I glanced at Tammy, who pushed out her lips and nodded in agreement. I was glad we only had to go as far as Chicago.

And Kate still wasn't done. "Plus, those heavy shoes you wear are real worn, Alex. You're gonna need to get a new pair and get them soon, so you can break 'em in good."

I pushed some food around my plate.

"Alex, you want work?" Bailey mumbled. "I have three families who always want me to sit for them on Wednesdays, so if you want, I can suggest you for one of those?"

"Really? That be great. Thanks, Bay Leaf."

Two days later, Bailey and I walked down to a house by the lake, and she introduced me to a family of doctors she used to sit for. They were both in their late thirties, with two kids, age six and three.

And just like that, I had my first job. It was super easy. The kids were asleep by the time I arrived at seven-thirty, and the docs were home at eleven-thirty. The whole time, I sat there eating chips and binging on Netflix. It was actually awesome to have that kind of peace and quiet away from Lucas and Kate. Tammy's house was so small compared to the mansion the riches lived in.

When they came home, I got thirty bucks plus a ten-dollar tip. It was awesome. They were very thankful and booked me in for that following weekend. They also recommended me to their neighbors, and before I could say boomshackalackaboom, I was working one school night a week and every Friday. It was awesome.

Chapter 35

I was in such a good mood that I decided to kiss Don. We hadn't seen much of each other because he was studying lots during lunch at school, but we texted back and forth a little.

Sunday afternoon I met him for milkshake at the Steak'n'Shake. I dropped so many hints about this new movie I wanted to see, and finally, just before we left, he said, "Hey, if you aren't doing anything, maybe we could go catch that movie?"

I sighed with relief. "Good thinking, Brain. It starts at seven-thirty. See you there."

Then came the hard part. I had to ask Snake-Eyes for a favor. We had been slowly developing a working relationship, and I figured after she had gotten me babysitting work, I could at least ask. Bailey was in her bedroom, emo music turned up loud. I knocked, and she didn't answer, so I just shouted as loud as I could. "Bailey, I'm coming in. You've got five seconds to hide whatever illegal stuff you're doing."

I slowly counted to five and entered. She was at the end of her bed, painting her toe nails. She held up a bottle of black polish.

"Go on, take some, Al. This is the good stuff." That was followed by her resident sarcastic smirk.

"So Bailey, you know how we're like best buds now? I need a favor. Can you watch Lucas later?"

Bailey concentrated hard on her painting, but her face was proper, like a madam, her lips pert. After a second, she looked up at me and blinked elegantly.

"You're going out with your little boyfriend, aren't you?"

"Ugh." I sighed, wishing I hadn't bothered. "He's not my boyfriend."

"Right, but you're going somewhere with him on a date, aren't you?"

"It's not a date."

"But it's the weirdly looking kid who is kinda hot, right?"

I rubbed my face with both hands and wondered how to get through this. Bailey wouldn't let up. "You are going somewhere with this weird-faced boy, probably somewhere safe and quiet and dark where you can make out. Am I right?"

"Bailey, can you frickin' do me this solid or not?"

She nodded and made this sexy face at me with catlike paws.

"But I want all the dirty details, babe."

"Ugh." I grunted and muttered thanks and got out of there.

At the movies, I felt so sleepy and relaxed. Don did a goofball yawn and put his arm around me and eventually kissed me, and I let him. He walked me home, and we kissed some more. He had matured over the past weeks, but his inexperience when it came to kissing was evident. He was noisy with too much spit, and it actually made me wanna puke.

"Don, this is pretty new," I said, all casual. "Maybe you wanna keep your tongue in your own mouth for now, hmm? I think that would be best. Or if you want, I'm cool with just holding hands." I shrugged nonchalantly.

Poor guy blushed. He knew he was gorgeous, but I didn't want his ego to grow any bigger than his tongue.

Chapter 36

The next few weeks were exhausting as I focused on training for my first Prizewinner feis. I was dancing two hours every night after school and more at weekends. On top of that, I was babysitting, doing school work and hanging out with Don every chance I got.

The dances were tough. My light shoe technique, which was normally excellent, was suffering because of the more complex steps and longer dances. I was feeling under pressure. Mrs. Gallagher had said that going to Oireachtas depended on how my next feis went. I was pushing myself hard, and at Thursday's dance class, I felt a tweak in my calf. I hoped it was nothing, but the following day, I was hobbling hard. Tammy gave me anti-inflammatory gel, and I iced it red that evening and after school on Friday, and I rested.

Mrs. Gallagher picked Kate and me up for Sunday's feis in Akron—home of LeBron. Kate wanted to come on the off-chance LeBron all of a sudden took an interest in Irish dance.

Things did not go my way from the outset. Even during warm up, I knew my leg was going to be a problem, and my energy seemed off. It was my first time competing against thirty girls, and I had to dance with two other girls on stage at the same time. I had no experience of this and spent the whole time trying to keep out of the way, but everywhere I wanted to go, they seemed to want to go also. It made concentrating so difficult, and on top of that, with my sore calf, the whole thing was a bust.

I ended up finishing outside the top twenty and tried my hardest not to start crying. If that wasn't bad enough, I overheard some girls talking about Oireachtas registration. One girl told me that the deadline for registering had been mid-September. I had missed the deadline, and besides all that, I wasn't good enough.

Mrs. Gallagher saw me welling up.

"Too bad, Alex." She sighed as she stood in front of me. "Take it easy on yourself. If anything, you've been working too hard. Why don't you take a week off?"

"A week off? I may as well quit. You said Oireachtas depended on how well I did..."

Mrs. Gallagher closed and opened her eyes slowly, and her face fell kindly to one side.

"You can still come to Oireachtas."

"Huh?"

"You can come. Providing you can pay your way, of course. Besides, Lucy would like the company." She smiled.

I shook my head furiously and sniffled. "But no, 'cause of the registration. The deadline. It's passed!"

To my surprise, Mrs. Gallagher grinned wide enough to fit a whole donut in her mouth. She spotted Kate and called her over.

"Kate, come here. I think now's the time you tell Alex a little secret." Kate looked at Mrs. Gallagher, unsure. "Go on now...about Oireachtas."

"What? What are you guys talking about?"

Kate rolled her head around, swinging her pony.

"Well, I had this idea a few weeks ago, and I told Mom. I knew for registration you had to be registered early, and when you came, you were all sad, so I said to Mom we should sign Alex up, and Mom said it wasn't a good idea, but I told her she was wrong. And then I gave her all my money from my piggy bank, and after Mom nearly cried, she said ok."

"That's right," said Mrs. Gallagher. "And when I saw how dedicated you were and Tammy explained how you might never get another chance to go to a major, we agreed to register you."

"Oh my gosh," I said, holding back tears of happiness as I hugged Kate. "Thank you so much," I whispered.

"So go easy on yourself. You're doing great for a beginner. Just keep working hard every day. And save up all that feis money for Chicago," said Mrs. Gallagher.

I nodded and made a decision not to bother with any more feiseanna until Chicago.

Kate dragged me towards the main stage. "I want you to see some of the girls dancing in Open. I know you didn't dance your best today, and I know you can do lots better, but you need to see just how much better you're gonna have to get."

"Wow, thanks Kate. Thanks for the pressure. Didn't Mrs. Gallagher just say take it easy?"

"Oh, forget her," said Kate with a dismissive wave of her hand.

"They are pretty good," I said as we watched the hornpipe. Kate did that thing she always did when I said something she didn't concur with. She blew a fart noise.

"Alex, look more closely. Look at the girl in the green and yellow. She's so flat-footed, it's crazy. Yeah, she does other good things, but she can't even get up on her points."

I shrugged my shoulders. "Well, I guess I can beat her then."

"But she keeps in time, always. She won't even be going to Oireachtas. You're going to have to beat girls like Erin Blake and Natasha Weevil, Noirin Valdes, Rochelle McGlynn. And of course, Jessica Harvey."

"Ohhh, frightening," I said sarcastically.

Her face stretched, and her eyebrows were popping off her face. She grabbed my cell and started playing with it. "Alex, you don't even have Instagram or Snapchat?"

"Those things suck, Katie."

She went ahead and installed the apps whether I liked it or not. She set up a profile and took a pic of me with a goofy smile in my black outfit. Then she forced phone under my nose.

"Look at Jessica's page," said Kate, scrolling through her pictures. I felt really dumb about my profile picture right then. Kate played a video clip of Jessica winning some competition. She really was a gorgeous dancer. She looked like the human version of Ariel from *The Little Mermaid,* with this tiny face, huge orange-chocolate eyes, white-white skin and a body to die for.

"I hate this girl, Katie, get her out of my face."

"You better get used to her, because she's the world title holder ever since when, and she's gonna be the one you have to beat by the time you're eighteen."

"Oh yeah? Well, maybe she'll suffer a horrible sickness and die by then."

"Even if she does, take a look at Erin."

Kate showed me five other dancers that were amazing, and these guys were just the North American posse. The Irish girls were just as good, and one from Scotland was another big deal. All of a sudden, I felt very worried about my heavy shoe dancing.

We waited around to watch Rochelle McGlynn. She went to a rival school in Cleveland called MasterStep, which was run by a brother and sister who used to perform with *Passion of the Dance*.

"She's so good." said Kate. "And the best part is, she's not a brat like some of them."

***

Later that day, Donald came over with pizza and ice cream, and we ate in the bedroom. He smiled like a goofball the whole time whenever there was silence. I could have found it annoying, but he was just way too easy to look at. He was a boy in a man's body.

It was a wonderful autumnal day, so we rode our bikes to Lakewood Park. The place looked amazing after all the renovations. They had built huge megalithic-style steps into the side of the cliff that zigzagged all the way down to the water, and there were all sorts of concentric circle stones that lined up just so when the sun rose on the summer and winter solstices. There were swings all along the shore for people to sit and watch the sun rise and set.

"Your dreams are starting to come true. I hear Oireachtas is lots of fun," said Don.

"Yeah, I guess."

"I was thinking about it. With everything that's going on with your grandpa, maybe your cousin is right. If you can become a professional dancer and get noticed, you can make a living for yourself. You can take care of yourself and Lucas. But in order for that to happen, I believe you have to do everything in your power to stay in Cleveland. Think about it. You have a dance class here and security, someone to care for you and bring you to feiseanna…"

"Oh yeah? You sure you're not just saying that 'cause you want me to stay and get in my pants?" I smirked.

Don almost choked. "No, I'm not saying it because… God, Alex, no, that's not the reason. Gosh, I would never just say something for that reason. No. No!"

"Relax," I laughed. "Well, thanks for the advice, Brain, but I don't really submit to that pipedream BS, you know?"

"All I'm saying is, I hope it works out for you to stay."

He said those words with the saddest eyes, and I couldn't help but wrap my arms up around his neck and kiss him long and soft.

Chapter 37

One day as Bailey and I made dinner, the phone rang. My fingers were covered in flour and egg mix as I dipped chicken strips for frying. Bailey, as usual, had her headphones in and couldn't hear. I kept making animated faces at her and nodding toward the phone, but she ignored me, smiling and dancing around while chopping veg. With no other options available, I kicked her in the shin.

"Ow, you stupid shit. What you do that for?" she asked, rubbing her leg. She took the ear buds out, and the phone went on ringing and ringing. She was fuming, and I tried not to laugh. I made an innocent face.

"The phone," I said, and held up my gooey white hands in defense.

Bailey grunted and answered the phone, which was on the kitchen table.

"Hello, hello, what could you possibly want?" Bailey grunted.

I laughed hard until Bailey's face changed complexion and her eyes widened toward me. The person on the other end must have kept talking, 'cause Bailey was quiet until finally she said, "I'm sorry, they're not in right now. Bye."

She pressed the end call button real hard, placed the phone carefully on the table, stared at it like it was about to blow, then gently blew hair out of her face. She smiled disingenuously at me and returned to her chopping, ear buds back in place.

"Who was that?" I asked. She ignored me. Finally, I tugged the wire from her iPod.

"Bailey," I said, this time with ferocity. "Are you going to be an ass all your life? Who was that?"

"It's not important. Make the chicken. Have I told you I looooove your chicken?" she said with a hopeful smile. But I punched her in the arm. "Ow, ok, ok. Sheesh, relax man."

She held the chopping knife upright like some kinda killer and spoke gently. "It's nothing to worry about. It was Debby."

"Mom?" I screeched.

"Yeah."

"And what? What did she say?"

"Look Al, what I'm about to tell you, don't let it bother you, because like everything is going to be alright."

"Bailey, enough trash, out with it."

Bailey spoke with her version of my accent.

"She said she was gonna come up to Cleverland and I'm taking back ma childers, or some BS like that. Then she said something about lawyers."

"Jesus Christ," I said real slow.

"But like I said. You're here and everything's great, and when you do go back, you'll be with Grandpa, so it doesn't matter right?" Bailey added with a quick smile.

My mind went woozy. I washed my hands under the cold water, and they didn't really rinse good, but I didn't care. Then I dried them on my sweater.

"I'm going out for some air."

Bailey's face was kind. "Sure. Take your time. I got this."

I went straight out the front door and started walking. Just as I left, Bailey yelled almighty.

"Kate? Get your butt in here."

I walked directionless, my mind swimming with crazy thoughts. Mom was bat-shit crazier than ever, and she was determined to make life hard. After we went back to Grandpa, she was gonna try all sorts of crazy. She was gonna wait her chance and abduct Lucas or something equally nuts. She would sooner see us all dead than not have things her way.

I walked blind for twenty minutes and finally realized I was only a couple blocks from Don's house. I rang his doorbell, and he answered.

"Alex, man, are you ok?"

And I just hugged him, and he held me for a moment at the door before leading me inside. Instinctively, he started making coffee, understanding enough to know I would talk when ready. His mom and dad were watching TV in the living room. Don led me to the basement, where they had another couch and TV.

Eventually, I told him that Mom had called. His reaction was so dramatic, shaking his head, saying, "Oh man, that's tough. Oh god."

But talking it out and having him to caress my hair and listen made me feel better. He held me on the couch, occasionally kissing the top of my head, and I began to relax.

"I guess you were going to have to face her at some point. She has no legal grounds to reverse anything. If you can hold her off for a couple years, I'll be your attorney." He grinned.

"Oh, no," I said, jumping up, realizing. "I'm so sorry Don. I should go and let you study."

"It's fine. I need a break anyhow. Besides, I like spending time with you. You can stay an hour."

He switched on a Netflix show that we barely watched, choosing instead to kiss a little. Then he walked me to the end of the block, and we said goodnight.

Chapter 38

I was able to put all thoughts of Mom to the back of my mind because all hell broke loose the week before Halloween. It all started when Kate, who was putting up new speed records in her special boot, came tumbling through the bedroom door, iPad in hand.

"Alex, you gotta see this." Her face was sparkling with excitement. She sat on the bed beside me, swiping and tapping like crazy. "Check it out."

She played a video clip of Kal McGettigan. He was in a dance studio, standing in his bare feet, wearing black shorts and tee. The clip was only fifteen seconds long, but I could see that it had been viewed over ten thousand times. Kate pressed play.

"Hey everyone, Kal here. Just wanted to check in with you guys. The past few months have been super busy, and it's almost time I let you in on a secret. My team and I have been working hard on various exciting projects, one of which is ready to go. For those of you with talent and ambition, I can tell you I'll be in Chicago for Oireachtas this November. I'm not going to tell you exactly what's going on just now; you guys can wait a couple more weeks, right? Let me say this much—I'll be auditioning boys and girls aged eight to eighty during Oireachtas week." He said that with a big white grin. "I promise to reveal all as soon as auditions are up and running. So everyone, keep practicing hard and see you in a couple weeks. Keep dancing and dream big. Bye."

Kate's mouth was wide open, and her palms were upturned as she looked hard at me.

"It's unbelievable, Alex, right?"

My eyes fell off to the side, not quite as enthusiastic. "I mean, I guess…It's not like he said anything we didn't already think."

Kate became annoyed. "No, you're wrong, Alex. This is huge." She squealed.

Just then, my cell rang. It was Lucy.

"Did you hear? He's got to be putting together a new show."

"Ugh, Lucy, you too?" I grunted. "He said dancers aged eight to eighteen — like what? He's putting together some kind of Irish dance circus? C'mon, Lucy, chill out. This is no BFD."

"Oh, Alex, lighten up. You could be totally wrong about this. Aren't you at least going to audition? I am. I so definitely am."

"I can't audition. I'm just a beginner, Lucy," I said flatly.

"Sure you can. Yeah, you're a beginner, but you're a nice dancer. What's the harm, right?"

"Meh, I guess I'll think about it."

After I hung up on Lucy, Kate told me to change into my dance gear to prep, and even though I thought it was totally over the top, I went to the garage with her for forty minutes. By the end, her infectious babbling had won me over. I had the biggest smile on my face, with dumb thoughts of being a star performer in Kal's new show, and dancing for hundreds of people printed like a vivid picture in my mind's eye.

Chapter 39

I was kind of torn as it got closer to Halloween, because a large part of me wanted to hang out with Don and another part of me knew I had so much practice to do and I didn't know how to prioritize it all according to the gospel of Nellie. Don had a similar problem in that his SATs were the first week in November, and he was putting in eight hours of study. He said if it was possible, we would hang out on Friday night.

But all work and no play was not working out for me. One day after a tough dance session, I decided to text Nellie. I had barely sent the message when she replied. We arranged to go for a walk in the park, and she insisted I bring Lucas.

We rode our bikes towards the lake and tied them at the bike stand next to the pool. Nellie, her hair now totally black but shaved tight on one side, waited with coffees and a backpack full of goodies. It was a little breezy but not cold. We set a blanket under one of the bare trees and got to munching chips and dip and chocolate. Lucas took to Nellie like nobody's business and cuddled into her as she fed him chips dipped in chocolate goo.

After a while, he went running after squirrels, and I told Nellie everything about Oireachtas and Kal McGettigan and kissing Don and whatnot. It was typical of her to just want to know more about this Don guy, and the more I talked about him, the more I realized how much I actually liked him. She told me that if I ever needed to make a little extra money to buy dance stuff, she could always talk to her boss in Novo. I thanked her for the offer. She said it was pretty fun to work there and that I would make lots of cool new friends.

After two hours, Lucas and I went home. Nellie was a great gal and such fun to hang out with.

***

On Friday night, Miller High had a home football game, and that was usually a big deal for all the kids. Bailey often got her face and arms painted and went with her friends, but I had never even considered it. Sitting through three hours of jocks being jocky was not my scene.

To my surprise, Don called me up straight after school.

"Alex, I can't take much more reading. It's like my eyes are about to burn holes through the next book I pick up. You wanna go to the game?"

"Oh Don, please say you're kidding?"

"C'mon, Alex, you've been dancing lots and I've been studying lots. It totally helps the brain to switch things up from time to time."

I conceded to his wishes, and to my surprise, we ended up having a really good time. We hung out with Bailey's friends at a guy called Lewis's house. They drank a couple of beers, but Don and I politely declined.

The game itself was kinda exciting mainly because Don held me close to him and kept me warm and we talked a lot.

"I can't understand why you wouldn't at least audition. You may never get another chance."

"But I'm a total newbie. Kal McGettigan doesn't want beginner dancers. How would that make sense?"

"How can you know what he's thinking?" said Don, getting annoyed. "What day do you dance, anyway?"

"Um, I think Under Fifteens are Saturday."

"And auditions?"

"I dunno, let me call Lucy."

I dialed her number, but she didn't answer.

"She could be here. Maybe we'll catch her later," I said.

"Yeah, well, you should aim to compete and aim to audition."

"And you should aim to worry about your own self, ok, Brain?" I said, and kissed him quickly on the cheek.

At Tuesday's dance class, Mrs. Gallagher had me focusing on my heavy shoe dancing as I tried to conquer the rhythm. I was working plenty on my technique, especially turning out my feet and getting up on my feet when I was supposed to. I had been doing lots of sit-ups and planks every morning, and days when I wasn't dancing, I rotated running and sprinting to help my endurance so I could see out my dances strongly. When I got a chance, I talked to Lucy.

"Hey, so these dumb auditions you keep talking about. When are they?"

"So the competition starts Friday, and I read on Kal's website that they will be auditioning Friday from three PM right through until Sunday evening. It's like a first-come, first-serve thing, so we should be fine. I'm gonna try and get mine done Friday evening, when I get there."

"So you mean any old chump can audition, all you gotta do is line up and wait your turn? Like, a grandma could wait in line and go in there and jump around and try and get in his show? No top twenties only?"

Lucy rolled her eyes. "He didn't really mean eighty-year-olds. That's just Kal…"

"That's just Kal?" I yelped. "Oooh, soorrry! Hate to impinge on you and your boyfriend's project, honey!"

Lucy pretended to be offended. "You're such a meanie."

Later that night, I counted up my savings from the babysitting jobs. I still a ways to go, because the Conrad Hotel where the competition was taking place was so expensive. Plus, every time Don and I hung out, I dipped into my money to buy food and pay for cinema tickets and whatnot. He always offered to pay for everything, but that wasn't how I rolled.

I had managed to block out Kate's jibber-jabber about dresses until one night, when she threw me with airplane talk.

"What you mean, airplanes?" I asked, putting a finger up against her lips to shush her.

"You don't have to take the airplane, you can go by train or bus too."

I smacked myself in the forehead. "Oh, no!"

I had no idea how I would get to Chicago. For some reason, I had thought Tammy and Kate would come, and then realized how stupid I was to think that. I ran into the kitchen and grabbed the iPad from the table and started searching. The cheapest flights were almost three hundred bucks return. The bus was always an option, but I knew Tammy would never allow that. But I had to try.

That night after dinner, I sat down with Tammy. I bit my lower lip and looked at her timidly. "Tammy, I'm going to Oireachtas, you know? I'm going to have to take the bus by myself."

Tammy opened her mouth to interrupt, but I spoke over her at great speed, becoming more assertive as I went on. "I checked flights, but they are out of my budget. So it's totally fine. I'll take the bus to downtown Chicago and have an Uber bring me straight to the hotel, and I promise not to leave the hotel until I'm going straight back to the Greyhound, so there's nothing to worry about, you know?"

Tammy had given up and smiled across at me. "I've organized with Joan that you and Lucy travel together. It's only like five hours, no big deal. Plus, you girls dance on the same day, so it makes sense. It also means you only pay for the hotel Friday night."

"Really?" My eyes widened. "Awesome, Tammy." I held out my hand for a high five.

"So you should really listen to what Kate has to say about getting some proper accessories, especially if you are saving money on travel."

"Ugh." I grunted.

"You need a dress and wig." She frowned.

"But doesn't a secondhand dress still cost like three or four hundred bucks? I only have like, a little to spare once the hotel and registration is paid for."

"Let's have a look right now, shall we?"

We scoured the internet. There weren't too many dresses available in my budget and my size in the greater Cleveland area, and driving for any more than two hours was out of the question. We called up some people and organized to see a few options the following day. There was only one dress I liked, but when I tried it on, we could barely zip it up. My last chance was a dress that only cost fifty bucks. It was so old fashioned I felt my bones ache and my back groan as I tried it on. It was long, down to my knees, where it was pleated, and it had all the colors in the world.

I wanted to say it was a horrible, black, shiny velvet dress, but that would not do it justice. There was also lots of yellow, orange, purple and blue. There was this disgusting Claddagh ring embroidered near the waist and a little pot o' gold-type thing for added Irishness. All the colors were strips of fabric sown onto the original black, and there were strips and strips of diamonds stuck on for fun. When I tried it on, I understand how it would make you a better dancer, because it was so goddamn itchy you really felt like jumping and dancing to forget the pain.

Those were the dresses pros. It was also baggy on me. Around the neck, there was embroidery of yellow, red, green and white. It was as if someone had spiked a toddler's drink and let it go wild with a sewing machine.

I whispered to Tammy. "I'll give you fifty bucks not to buy it." But the sellers threw in a crappy brown bun wig to seal the deal.

Kate was so excited to see me in my first ever dance dress, but when I modelled it in the kitchen later that night, her eyes filled with tears.

"Mom, I can't believe you made her get it."

Bailey literally rolled around on the floor laughing. "Oh jeez, Alex. You're gonna get killed."

"Tammy," I pleaded. "Can't you fix up this with your sewing machine?" I said pathetically.

She shook her. "Fraid not. You can't do anything with the dress the way it is now. Besides, I think it's cute."

It would have to do.

"Hate to say it, Al, but you're gonna have to sweet talk your way onto the podium, girl, 'cause no one's gonna see your moves. Just buy the judges a drink."

I bowed my head. Bailey was right. I would have to re-evaluate my hopes and dreams for Oireachtas.

Chapter 40

Halloween week Buck came home early from work with a bunch of flowers. Bailey and I felt bad 'cause neither of us had started making dinner, but when he saw us scamper he tutt-tutted and wagged his finger and told us to stay, like two pet dogs.

"What's going on, Dadge?" asked Bailey.

"Good news, that's what. We're having pizza."

When Tammy came home, she flopped onto the couch and closed her eyes, but we were all so excited, trying not to say anything until Buck came back with fizzy wine and a whole bunch of Halloween decorations. He popped the lid real loud and poured a surprised Tammy a glass. He knelt down beside her and kissed her deeply on the lips. Tammy's eyes glowed. Then he dumped the bag of decorations on the floor.

"This place ain't scary enough. Who wants to help?"

"I do!" screamed Lucas.

"Me too," said Kate.

Soon we were hanging spider webs and pumpkins with candles all 'round the house. At seven Buck opened a bottle of red wine, poured himself and Tam a glass, and soon three humungous pizzas arrived.

"What's all this for?" Kate asked.

"The good news is we now own this whole house!"

Everyone clapped and cheered.

"So I guess the stress is over now, right, Mom? You can start making dinners again?" asked Bailey.

"I wish. This is just the start. We are in debt to Grandpa and the bank for the next twenty years! Plus, the lawyers take forever."

"I'm not gonna worry about that right now," said Buck who went to the kitchen cabinet and pulled out his old pipe and some block tobacco from a metal box. Then he took his wine glass and headed outside. "I'm only in the mood for celebrating."

Tammy was being realistic. "We might not get the keys until Christmas time. Then the renovating gonna cost a whole lot more."

Lucas perked up at the mention of Christmas. "How many weeks until Christmas? It's gonna be such fun spending Christmas with Aunt Tammy and Mr. Buck."

"Yeah, it's gonna be so much fun," Kate squealed.

I exhaled quietly. For a moment, I had allowed myself to fantasize, and I'd pictured having my own room upstairs. But by Christmas time, both Lucas and I would be back with Grandpa.

"Will Santa Claus know to bring our presents to Lakewood?"

"'Course he will," said Kate. "Santa knows everything, doesn't he, Mom?"

I needed to change the conversation. It killed me to think that all the progress and good work Lucas and I had done in Lakewood would count for nothing and that we'd soon have to start another new life from scratch in Alderhill.

Chapter 41

On the Monday after fall break, I saw a familiar-looking kid by the secretary's office. I didn't think about it anymore until he walked into my second period math class. Then I realized.

It was Martin's brother, Declan. I had met him briefly at State Championships in Cincinnati. He was fifteen or sixteen, a couple inches taller than me, with a mischievous, slightly freckled baby-face disguised with some stubble. He had a mop of brown hair and glasses that were obviously just for fashion purposes.

I didn't get much of a look at him again until that Tuesday. I rocked up at dance class, and there he was, deep in conversation with Mrs. Gallagher. He spotted me warming up afterwards and came straight over.

"How's it going?" He smiled. He opened his arms for a hug. I awkwardly accepted. "You decided to take it up yourself, huh?" he said, nodding at my soft shoes.

"Yeah, nothing better to do."

"How's things?"

"Great," I lied. "What are you doing in Cleveland? You here for keeps?"

"Aye, my father was able to get a job and move over, and I was finishing up some exams and that in Ireland, so this was kinda the right time to move over. Mammy and Martin were here, so it was just a matter of when."

"Where are you staying?"

"We're in a wee house on Franklin Avenue, not far from the Beck Center."

"Cool, that's pretty close to my place."

"Sound. Well, I'd better get changed." He winked as he walked away. I wondered if that was weird or cool?

Again Mrs. Gallagher worked with me on my heavy shoe dancing. It felt like I had improved exponentially over the past six weeks. My core muscles were catching up with what I was asking them to do. I was now able to rally faster and twist and turn quicker while maintaining my balance. Rhythm was still a big issue, though.

I watched Declan practice as much as I could, because he was truly something else. I had seen clips on YouTube but seeing him in the flesh was another matter. He had complete control of every single move and technique, and he danced with fire. He was flawless.

As I sat down to untie my soft shoes, he came over, panting and slurping pink water.

"Mrs. Gallagher told me she's bringing you to Oireachtas. That'll be exciting."

"Yeah, it really is. Like I've only just started, so to get this chance is amazing. Are you going?"

He shook his head no. "Martin was telling me about you." He smiled again.

There was something about his smile that made me want to mimic his dumb accent, but I managed to stop myself. "Martin said you were improving lightning fast. He's right, you know," he said, nodding approvingly. "You've lovely feet."

I scrunched my nose and became very aware of how short my shorts were. He quickly corrected himself. "The way you dance like, not your actual legs." He smiled his smile again. "Like, your legs are nice too." Then he bit his lower lip and shook his head really quickly, blushing just a tiny amount. "Jaysus, ye can't say nothing these days for people taking it up the wrong way."

But I returned his grin.

He did a couple of neat tricks so fast in front of me, then spun around to walk away. He only made it a couple yards before he turned around.

"That *Storyteller* you're workin' on. It's pure shite."

"Huh?" I frowned.

"Will you be here on Thursday?" I nodded. "Aye, good. If its ok with yourself and Mrs. Gallagher, I have a few wee suggestions that might help make it flow a bit better."

"A few wee suggestions?" I frowned.

"Aye," he repeated. "Just a tweak here and there that will make it more effective for Oireachtas. Alright?"

"Ok, alright." I nodded uncertainly. But he wasn't done.

"There's beginner tap classes in the Beck Center on Fridays, by the way. It's only eight dollars drop-in fee. Would probably help you with your rhythm. Pilates might be good too. Just another wee suggestion." With that and a trademark wink, he was gone. "See you later, Alex."

***

I didn't see Declan after that until the following Thursday.

I skipped morning classes to bring Don a card I made wishing him good luck on his SATs, which he was taking later that day, before heading to school. As I made my way across the football field and gym to the main building, I happened upon a bunch of jocks making all sorts of childish noises and jumping around like hungry chimps. As I got closer, I saw that the source of their amusement was Declan.

One guy who was at least six-foot-five and wearing an orange Cleveland Browns hoodie threw a football right into Declan's face. They stood laughing and watched him rub his cheek, waiting to see what would happen next.

I stopped. Declan slowly bent down and picked up the ball, offered it back to the giant with one hand, then turned around and drop-kicked the football a mile toward the carpark. The tall guy and a shorter, mousey-faced kid approached, with two others hanging back. I was less than ten yards away and could hear everything.

"Best not mess with the leprechaun. He might pull out his lucky charms," said the shorter guy.

"Or worse, jig us all to death. Come on, Irish, let's see some of your moves." They circled round Declan like a couple of mosquitos. I looked around to see if there was anyone that could help and just for a second thought about calling Don but decided against it.

Declan didn't say anything or move. A third jock wearing an Indians hat joined and began doing his interpretation of Irish dancing.

Declan stood there in amazement. "Hey, you know what? That was actually quite good. Your elevation was very good, and you kept your back straight and your arms nicely by your side. Well done, chief."

"Shut your mouth, Irish," he replied, turning red.

Declan continued. "I'm being honest. If you went to classes, you might pick it up quick. Hundred percent."

The boys then took turns shouting homophobic slurs at Declan; he maintained complete coolness. I went up to Declan and nudged his elbow, trying to get him to follow me out of there, but he barely noticed me. His eyes were all white and fixed on the bullies.

"Are you boys actually simple or something?" Declan said finally.

"What did you call us?"

"What are you lads doing at school? Youse haven't two brain cells to rub together between the three of you."

Declan was cucumber-calm. The smaller jock didn't like that at all. He got right up in Declan's face, noses almost touching. At that point, I tugged harder at Declan's arm.

"Declan, I need you for a second. Why don't you guys back off?"

"Dude needs his girlfriend to come to the rescue," said the tall guy.

I had to use all my strength to drag Declan away. There was steam rising from his head. He mumbled to himself all the way up the steps into school. Finally, he turned to me.

"Cheers, Alex."

"Cheers?" I said back, confused, before realizing it was probably Irish code for thanks. "Oh yeah, sure. No problem. Just try not to get into anymore three-on-ones, Irish. Ok?"

As I walked away, I turned around. "You know, there's a Jujitsu class in the Beck Center every Thursday. It's like eight bucks drop-in. And I think they do mixed martial arts on Detroit and Nicholson. Just a suggestion."

Then I winked and kept walking, swinging my hips ever so gently, trying my best not to laugh out loud.

***

At the next dance class, Declan spoke with Mrs. Gallagher, and they came up to me afterwards.

"Declan wants to show you something to help your Storyteller set. That's ok by me if its ok by you?"

I nodded. "Yeah, sure, why not?"

"If it's too much for you, we don't have to stick with it, but you can give it a try."

Mrs. G. waddled away, leaving Declan and I to it.

"Ok, so I noticed last time you're good at some things and very good at others, like you're strong on your blocks and your double-clicks. So if we add in a twist and a few wee things, it will look a lot better. You'll score higher with the judges doing it this way than you would without."

Declan showed me a new spin, a double-click above my head and a run on my blocks. He said I was doing a good job, but it didn't feel that way to me. We worked a solid hour, and he was happy to keep going even after class had finished, but I was done.

"Thanks, man. That was pretty great."

"No problem. You still have a few weeks to get that nice. Good start."

Later I told Kate, who went berserk.

"I cannot believe Declan is teaching you. I'm coming to class next time. I want to see him dancing up close."

"Why do you think Mrs. Gallagher allowed him to change my steps?"

"They have way better teachers in Ireland and dance nicer steps. She probably knows Declan would be a better teacher than her. She will do anything he says. He's a world champion, remember?"

Chapter 42

Time was really flying by, and between school, dancing and hanging out with Don, who had 'successfully' completed the SATs, I hardly had a chance to take everything in.

Lucas was almost a stranger to me at Tammy's house. I got to see him for a bit after preschool, but the rest of the time, he had his own routine. He had a couple friends a few blocks away, and a mom would come pick him up and take him on play dates.

Fuzz called me one night to see how my Oireachtas preparations were going, so I updated him on everything. After that, I remembered there was another man in my life—went by the name Grandpa—who I hadn't spoken to in what seemed like ages. I picked up the phone and dialed Alderhill.

"Nice to hear from you, darling, how you been?"

"Real good, Grandpa. We're all doing great. How are you?"

"I'm doing good too. I'm getting stronger every day. I don't even need Peggy no more."

"You don't?"

"That's right. She's been gone two weeks now."

"Two weeks," I yelled. "But Grandpa, that's not—"

"That's right. Two weeks. I can do everything I once could even better than ever. The community nurse comes to check on me on a Tuesday and a Friday. Those social people have been real nice too. They sent some cleaners over to come get the house ready for you and Lucas. Place is like new."

"Really?" I squealed without realizing exactly what he was saying.

"Matter of fact, the lady is coming tomorrow. She says you guys are right and ready to come back here and live with me. Isn't that great? I was gonna wait until after tomorrow before callin'." Grandpa sounded so pleased, and I found myself matching his tone, but it was only in sound and not in spirit. Tammy came in just then with a bag of groceries, and I handed her the phone. "Grandpa's got news."

I went outside to sit on the swing. She spoke to him for another while, then the back door swung shut as she came out to me.

"Well, isn't that good news? Aren't you happy?"

I shrugged my shoulders.

"What's the matter, Alex? Isn't this everything you wanted?"

"I mean, I guess. But what about Oireachtas? Grandpa said we can go back tomorrow…"

Tammy's face changed as she understood. "Go back inside. It's cold out here."

***

The following day, Tammy came to me in the bedroom as I sat watching Netflix on Bailey's iPad.

"I talked with your grandpa again and told him about the competition in Chicago. It's only an extra two weeks. He said it's fine for you guys to wait until then."

"So you mean I can go to Oireachtas?"

Tammy nodded. I contained a scream and squeezed her hard.

The week before Oireachtas, Mrs. Gallagher drilled us into the ground. I had been practicing Declan's new steps like crazy, and we had dance class every day. Even though Declan wasn't going, he came to dance class every day to help Lucy and me. Declan was very pleased with how far along I had come in the space of two weeks.

"Nice job, Alex," He said. "You're very graceful, and it looks effortless. Well done."

Lucy and I stayed back an extra half hour and talked. I was so envious of her heavy dancing.

"I wish I had your rhythm," I said.

She blew a stray piece of hair out of her eyes. She had a new cut—it had been long, but now it curled around her ears. The styled lifted her face, and she looked much cuter.

"I wish I was as elegant as you," she retaliated.

"No seriously, you are all 'round perfect," I said.

She stopped what she was doing and shook her head. "No, no, you are."

Fearing it would turn into a battle of compliments, I quickly changed the tune.

"Ok, let's cut the BS. Just tell me how I conquer the rhythm."

She laughed. "Right. I guess it was never a problem for me, so I was lucky." I rolled my eyes, and she pointed sharply. "But! One thing that helps for sure is not thinking about it and pretending no one is there and really going for it."

I made a noise with my mouth and nodded. "Yeah, good one, Lucy, real helpful," I said sarcastically.

She laughed. "Dance the steps really slowly without the music and watch yourself in the mirror. Sometimes the music in your head needs to sync with the actual music, if you see what I mean?"

I nodded in agreement but said, "Yeah, Lucy, I have no clue what you mean. But thanks."

"So where are you hoping to finish?" she asked.

"I don't have a clue. I'm just excited to go."

"Your age group is tough. Jessica Harvey is a multiple world champ. She wins Oireachtas and Nans every year."

I nodded. "Kate keeps telling me about her."

"She's a real piece of work," said Lucy, making a face.

"You should have seen her at the masterclass."

Lucy rolled her eyes.

"You're probs still all excited about these auditions, right? You really believe Kal McGettigan's got a new show ready to roll out?"

Lucy's eyes grew. "I dunno. But some of the girls on Facebook were saying it could be a small touring show with kids straight out of college."

"College kids? Why?"

"I guess 'cause he can pay them less to dance? I dunno. I don't care either. Just pick me! Pick me!" she wailed, and laughed. "I'm more excited about the auditions than I am Oireachtas. We will have to try and get them done the first night, seeing as we're driving home after we dance on Saturday." She looked past me into the distance, making goofy eyes towards the heavens. "Imagine. We'll be driving home celebrating winning Oireachtas and getting picked for his new show."

Mrs. Gallagher came over and ran me through my set dance.

"It's looking real nice now, Alex. Those moves Declan gave you make it look great. I think you might do ok."

I went home and thought about everything and felt strangely melancholic. It was potentially my first and only major, and I had just danced my final class at Rocky River with big old Gallagher and Lucy and all the little sprites. I practiced until two AM in the garage doing as Lucy said—really going for it with my heavy dancing, doing that thing I had become accustomed to when I didn't want to fully think about my life and its changes.

Tiredness finally caught up with me. I fell heavy into bed.

Chapter 43

Everyone including Bailey wished me luck and
waved me goodbye on Friday early afternoon when I got
in the car with Lucy and her mom to go to Chicago.
Lucas asked if I was coming back but didn't seem to
mind—he looked so content by Tammy's side. Kate
hobbled after as I got into the car.

"Good luck, Alex. This is step one of our goal,
remember?" she said with a glint in her eye.

I didn't feel nervous until we arrived at the hotel in
Chicago. I'd thought it would be similar to State Champs
in Cincinnati, but I'd been way off. It was enormous.
There were thousands of kids and adults coming and
going. We got there just before nightfall, with both of us
due to dance first thing Saturday. Tammy made sure I
gave Joan a hundred bucks for gas.

After checking in, Lucy got changed into her practice
gear. She wanted to get her audition done before her
competition the next day. I wasn't sure if I wanted to
audition and decided to see how I felt the following
morning, but I did go with her to the third floor, where
Kal and his team had booked a function room to hold
auditions.

As soon as the elevator doors opened, both our jaws
just smacked off the carpet. There wasn't even room to
get out—it was like a floor jammed with Irish dance
sardines of all ages and sizes, waiting in line. Poor

Lucy's face was like a momma bird who had watched her young being eaten by a cat. I grimaced and stayed in the lift as she tried to squeeze out.

"Good luck with that, Lucy. I'll see ya around."

I hung out in the room and texted Don for a while. Lucy came back after eight.

"Well?" I said, hopeful. Lucy threw her phone on the floor and flopped onto the bed.

"Come back tomorrow. That's what they said."

That night Lucy and I did our tan, and Joan fixed our hair as we watched TV. We turned the lights out at ten, but I was so wired I couldn't fall asleep, whereas Lucy was out cold the second she lay down. The following morning, she was up and messing around just after five. And her slightest movements were enough to wake me.

"Jesus, Lucy," I croaked. "Where are you going?"

"I'm gonna check to see if they are auditioning."

"You've lost it, girl. This is sabotage. You're going to kill all of our chances."

I closed my eyes for another twenty minutes, but it was no use, and after Lucy's terrible attempt to sneak back into the room without waking me—she knocked over a glass that smashed into a million pieces—I knew sleep was out of the question.

At that point, I didn't care about dancing. I dragged Lucy to breakfast, which was a buffet situation with all the most delicious fried foods and healthy stuff. I drank three cups of coffee and immediately felt better. Lucy ate a pear.

Lucy's mom joined a big line to collect our numbers and programs at seven-fifteen, while Mrs. Gallagher took Lucy and me to the practice floor for warm up. I was due to dance after eight AM, which gave me under an hour to get ready. Lucy and I were basically dancing at the same time except in different ballrooms, which would make it difficult for Mrs. Gallagher to watch and help out.

"I'll do my very best to be there for both you girls, but these halls are long and busy, and I'm not as fit as I once was."

It was true. She was heavier than the first time I had met her. "But I believe in both you girls, and I know you'll do us all proud." She smiled.

She drilled me through my hornpipe over and over again until I was so sweaty. I went outside to cool off and patted myself dry with a towel. At ten minutes to eight, I put the dreaded dress on. I looked ridiculous and felt so self-conscious, standing out like a complete idiot.

I had changed. Once upon a time, I hadn't given a damn about what anyone thought or said about me, but since I'd started Irish dancing, that had changed. I needed some old Alex back. But my stomach was feeling flaky and nervous since I'd come downstairs, especially when I noticed I was number 217; the hornpipe round was starting at number 202. I also needed to pee every ten minutes because of all the water I had drunk.

Lucy's competition was slightly behind schedule, so we watched the first few dancers in my competition before running back to the foyer to mark out my hornpipe steps one final time. Watching my competitors practice in the foyer made me feel utterly useless — some of them were so precise. After a few run-throughs, Lucy high-fived me.

"Cheer up, Alex. You'll do great."

But the dress was kind of speaking to me in a hushed voice, telling me otherwise.

"I'll be back soon as I can. Good luck."

Lucy left me there all alone to cower in the shadows. All I could feel were stares pouring from strangers' eyes. It was way harder to practice by myself, feeling so self-conscious. Just as I was about to go inside the hall and line up, my ears tuned into a group of girls standing nearby. Three girls were laughing, pointing, making weird voices and being generally obnoxious. One of the girls looked familiar. She was wearing a white dress and a long, black wig, but her face was tiny. She looked like a doll. We made eye contact briefly before I got back to my carpet staring business.

But soon there was an "Oh My God", and I knew it was aimed at me.

"Hey girls, check it out. This is a real piece of nostalgia we're seeing here."

Her girls laughed hard.

"Holy shit," one of them said.

The girl in the white dress came toward me. "Lainy, you got your phone? I gotta get a picture with this."

I was too startled and nervous and shy about my dress to know what to do.

"Hey sweetie, you don't mind, do ya? If we get a pic? I'm Jessica. I don't think we've met."

"Um, Alex," I said, and shook her hand. I hated myself for doing so.

"Nice to meet you, sweetie." She smiled fake politeness. "You sure you're in the right place? Just kidding!"

"Um, I think so."

"Oh wow, a southern belle? You def don't belong here. Ok, Lainy, shoot."

She put her arm 'round me and made a goofy smile and cheered, and her friend took a picture.

"So, good luck with that," she said, looking me over and rejoining her friends. After that, they laughed so hard, looking at the picture and making comments that I tried to block out.

I didn't want to dance anymore. I went into the hall and lined up with the girls I would be on stage with.

Watching the girls on stage dance turned my stomach, and I wished I hadn't eaten all that breakfast. They were so unbelievably good and confident, and there were tons of them. I started freaking out, and my heart was beating all the way up in my temples. As I looked down at myself, I wondered who I was, with the stupid costume and fake tan, and how I had ended up here, ready to make a fool of myself in front of hundreds of people.

As I looked back and forth for an escape, I saw a little boy, blonde and about Lucas's age, and a different feeling took over. Images floated in, and I held them in front of my mind's eye in bright colors. I imagined Lucas and I staring out at the lake, the sun beating down hard, feeding warm nourishment into our hearts.

With that, I forced myself to breathe like a relaxed human being. I was still jittery and lightheaded but slowly feeling better. As the final group before mine went up, I decided not to watch and stared at the swirly-colored carpet instead. I spent some time reminding myself that I enjoyed dancing, and because I was doing what I loved, there was no need to worry. And as I followed the girls in my group, I heard that voice again from a little farther down my line.

"Good luck, southern belle. I hope you fall. Jokes!"

I clenched my teeth.

It was hard to concentrate after that. I floated up the steps onto the stage, and everything was just bright lights and noise, and the robotic part of my brain sent me through the motions. I swallowed hard to keep the vomit from coming up.

Then the music began, and I calmed myself with long exhales and gritted my teeth and tried to do as I had done hundreds of times in the garage and at dance practice. I had no actual idea how I danced because I was in such a weird trance. It was totally overwhelming. I was so busy trying to keep out of the other two girls' way; they seemed hell bent on dancing in front of one particular judge stage left, where I had started.

Somehow I made my way across to the opposite side and had the whole place to myself, and I think — or at least it felt like — my dancing got stronger, and I finished it out well. Before I knew it, the hornpipe was over and I was bowing in front of the judges, trying to remember to smile. I came off stage panting, as if waking from a drowning experience, sucking air. Jessica Harvey put her arm out to catch my attention as I passed. She was bobbing and weaving her head like a gangster rapper.

"This shit is mine!"

Mrs. Gallagher came trundling toward me.

"How did you do?"

"How did I do? What do you mean? You didn't see it?"

"No, I just got here."

I felt pretty crappy that my dance teacher had not made a bigger effort to come watch me dance and support me in my first ever major competition.

"I honestly have no clue, Mrs. Gallagher."

She looked at me with sad eyes. "Well, you made it back down here in one piece. That's a good start, right, honey?" she said, attempting a smile.

Chapter 44

After that, I changed into my soft shoes and drank a gallon of water as the sweat dripped down my back and forehead. I really wanted to take the heavy piece-of-crap dress off and knew that a simple black skirt would have been much better. Mrs. Gallagher must have felt bad that she had missed my dance, 'cause she was super supportive after that. She brought Lucy and I across the hotel grounds to the main part of the hotel and bought us a cup of tea and a chocolate bar.

Lucy was very pleased with how she had danced. I told her all about Jessica.

"Wow, she really is a giant turd, isn't she?" said Lucy.

"I know, right? Man, she doesn't know a thing about karma."

In the middle of my sentence, Lucy gripped my arm and froze.

"Don't look now."

Instinctively, I went to turn around, but Lucy slapped me hard on the leg and pierced my skull with her stare.

"Don't look. Keep talking like we're having a really important conversation."

Then she started into some really bad play-acting, nodding her head like she was on a news panel. I burst out laughing in her face just as Mrs. G. landed back and alongside her.

Dressed in jeans and a white tee and a sports jacket with his hair slicked back was Kal McGettigan.

"Girls, Kal wanted to come and say hi," said Mrs. Gallagher.

"Alex, so good to see you. It's amazing to hear how much you've progressed. How did your hornpipe go?" Kal was being polite, but his cheeks were red.

"Um, uh," I stammered. "Actually, I can't remember!" Then I burst out laughing, because to say that to a guy of such power and prestige seemed disrespectful. To my amazement, he laughed straight back.

"Excellent. That happened to me a couple times. Guess that's what happens when you just go out there and enjoy it."

Then he looked at Lucy. "Hi, Lucy. Good to see you take on board some of my suggestions. You danced very nicely earlier."

Lucy mouthed a shy 'thank you'.

Then he looked back at me. "I'm taking a little break from auditions and leaving them to Diane and Frances." He made a little whistle and stared at the floor. "We are up to our eyes trying to get through everyone. I'm gonna go over to ballroom two for a bit. Good luck with the rest of your dances. Bye."

Then he kissed Mrs. Gallagher on the cheek and left.

Lucy was bright red, and Mrs. Gallagher was blushing so hard I started fanning her face with a program in case she might pass out.

"Oh, come on girls, untwist those panties now, ya hear? He's just any other guy, for Chrissake," I said.

"He knew your name, Alex," said Lucy in astonishment.

"He knew yours too," I sang.

"That's 'cause I was in his classes. He called you Alex!"

"Well duh, it's my name, ain't it?" I said, all smart. "And besides, he wrote me a letter last summer."

"What letter? Oh god, he loves you."

"Who doesn't, ya 'know?" I said with fake confidence as I blew my fingernails.

"Gosh, I hope there's a big break between now and recalls. I'm gonna run upstairs and audition."

Mrs. Gallagher gathered herself and cleared her throat.

"Girls, settle down." She shook her head at Lucy. "You're not to go anywhere until you've completed all your dances. I don't want either of you getting too big for your boots. I want complete focus."

She nodded her head in my direction. "Now off you go and get ready for your reel. I'll follow you girls over once I finish my tea."

***

As I warmed up for my reel, I was feeling so high on life and fun vibes. Mrs. Gallagher talked to me in really low tones and kept bringing my face back to her eyes.

"Alex, keep your breath regular now. You can use all this energy in a moment when you are on stage, but right now I want you to breathe and picture yourself dancing and delighting everyone with your steps, ok?"

But when she turned to Lucy, she made this big-eyed face. She was scared I was going to mess up. That's when I knew she was right. I had to ground myself. I exhaled low and long and tried my best to focus. But it was so hard. It was like I had drunk a gazillion espressos. And it was the reel, which was my favorite dance.

I spotted Jessica not too far away. She didn't have her gang this time and instead listened to her iPod. I didn't watch her dance and just focused on my breathing and thought about Lucas and Kate and Dad and even Mom. When it was time for my group to go on stage, I walked very slowly up the steps and took all the time in the world to suck in the crowd, the five judges, the lights, the atmosphere. And I was ready. Reels were my thing.

The music started, and it was a reel I loved. I allowed my body to float around in what felt like pure art, the leaps, the twists. I had drifted away. Adrenaline and dopamine took control as my body moved and my face smiled, teasing the judges, skipping side stage and into the ether. My heart was pounding strong and steady as we bowed. I had nailed it. Coming off stage, I heard people ask who I was. That made me feel amazing.

Mrs. Gallagher was pale as I walked towards her. She hugged me tight.

"Alex, you danced wonderfully. That's the best reel I've ever seen you dance. Come on outside, honey, and let's get you some air and water."

I felt woozy as she ushered me outside through all the people.

"You still can't remember how your hornpipe went, darling?"

"No, Mrs. Gallagher. It was a total blank, I was so nervous."

I started wondering if Mrs. Gallagher thought I had a chance of recalling but didn't want to ask.

There was a long time to wait around as all the other dancers danced their reels. I went to see if Lucy had danced yet, and she had, but I couldn't find her anywhere and figured she had probably sneaked upstairs to try and get her audition done.

I went to the room for a while, texting Kate and Don and watching a little TV. Lucy texted me to tell me she had been recalled and was getting ready to dance her set. I was ready to go watch her, but Mrs. Gallagher messaged to tell me they were announcing recalls. I ran to the elevator and went into the auditorium, not able to find her anywhere. A woman in a red dress stood side stage with a microphone and a sheet of paper.

"Here are the recalls for Under Fifteen girls."

She started calling out numbers, and I was somehow expecting names. Girls beside me started screaming and jumping around. Others started crying. My mind had blanked, and I had to look down at my crappy dress to remind myself I was number 217. And I felt so numb; my mind blurred as the numbers kept coming out. My heart was beating around in my chest like it wanted to escape. The lady called 207, and then she called 217 and 227 and 228 and 247 and carried on. I wasn't sure if I had heard what I thought I heard. I looked around all confused, and a mom must have noticed, 'cause she just smiled real sincere at me as she stood with her own weeping daughter and mouthed the words 'well done'.

And I almost lost my mind. Just then Mrs. Gallagher came bowling towards me.

"Oh my goodness, Alex." She kept saying it over and over, her chocolate breath in my face. "You have to go up to that lady now and tell her what set you're dancing and what speed you want it, ok, honey?"

Chapter 45

I hardly had any time to prepare for my set dance because the order of dancers was already fixed and I would be one of the first to dance. Lucy came running into the foyer, head spinning every which way until she spotted me.

"Alex, wow! I can't believe it," she said screaming in my ear. She checked the time on her phone. "Ok, let's get you ready."

"But what about your set?" I asked.

"I'm done. It went great," she said frankly.

She walked me to a quiet corner of the foyer near a large plant in a cube-shaped box. We passed Kal and Diane, who were staring into a small moleskin book, deep in discussion. I wondered if he had seen my reel. I wondered if he even knew I had been recalled. But their conversation ended as I sat on the carpet tying my laces. Kal went toward ballroom one, and Diane went the opposite way.

"What's on in there right now, Lucy?"

"Under Seventeen boys."

I made a face.

"Forget about that now, Alex. And no, no wait. Don't tie your shoes yet. Let's mark out your set in your socks first."

"Ugh, Lucy, why didn't you say that five minutes ago?" I groaned when one of the laces developed a knot.

Lucy bent down and fixed it for me. She was calm and serious. She had taken on a new role—mother, sister, mentor, friend, supporter. I didn't want to let her down. I'd only had around five-minutes practice when Mrs. Gallagher found us.

"It's time for you to line up. Deep breaths. Focus on nothing other than your steps and your performance, and everything will be fine."

Despite feeling inspired after dancing a great reel, I was more nervous than ever. During my first two rounds, I had danced with two other girls on stage, but now it would be just me and fourteen eyes watching my every miniscule movement. There would be no room for error or lapse in concentration.

I was so anxious waiting in line that I almost forgot to breathe, and I was becoming lightheaded, especially after watching the first girl dance. She started off really well, but suddenly after a leap, her ankle buckled to the side when she landed. She cried out so loudly that everyone could hear over the music. She somehow finished her dance, but straight after she bowed she burst into tears and hobbled real slow off stage, her hands covering her face. I started panicking, thinking that could happen to me.

Then it was me. Everything felt like a buzzy blur, so I closed my eyes for a second and pictured myself in the class at Rocky River, with Declan's mischievous smile and funny accent guiding my moves. I smiled a little. I remembered Tammy's words. *Attack the stage.*

It was time to make moves. I stood waiting for the music to play me in and licked my lips a little, remembering to smile, and as soon as I had danced my first few steps, it felt like I was growing wings. I made my way towards one particular judge, who had only a little black patch of hair 'round the sides, and saw him tapping his pen on his sheet, his face relaxed. That pushed me forward.

As I moved across to stage right, it felt like I was gliding. I felt happy. I felt relaxed. I loved how everyone's eyes were focused on me and everyone was silent. I was doing something I had loved since I was a kid — performing. The dance ended, and I took a slow bow, soaking it in, not giving a damn about my crappy dress anymore.

"Really nice, Alex. Declan worked wonders with you. Everything was clean and nicely executed," said Mrs. Gallagher.

Lucy intertwined her hand with mine and nodded with a little smile. "Really good, Alex. I'm so happy for you."

She seemed ready to stay by my side, but I turned to her. "Lucy, you've done too much for me already. I don't need you to stay. Go see about auditioning."

"Are you sure?" she asked with a scrunched, sad face.

I made my 'of course' expression back at her. I sat and rested and ate a sandwich that Mrs. Gallagher plonked onto my knee.

It was weird watching my competition. Some of the girls danced complicated and intricate steps with such precision that it was a shame to hope they messed up. When the familiar white dress of Jessica Harvey got on stage, I looked away. She got a round of applause after she had finished. She must have been so good. For a moment, I felt really annoyed with the Irish dancing world. Why did the recall dance have to be in heavy shoe?

Everything changed after Jessica danced. She seemed to curse the stage for everyone that came after — a comical series of misfortunes and disasters followed.

There was a great deal of anxiety in the hall that seemed to spread in the air like a poisonous chemical.

The girl who went right after Jessica slid so bad that she had to be helped off stage. There was another delay as a girl got sick in the bathroom. I noticed some girls actually high-fiving as their competitors got injured or disqualified. Jessica Harvey was openly laughing out loud with her buddies. It was disgusting.

The next girl finished ok but made mistake after mistake. Two more girls slipped on stage. Angry teachers approached the organizers and demanded the floor be cleaned and their students allowed to dance again. After much discussion, some cleaners inspected the dance floor and began dry mopping. I couldn't take it any longer and got out of there for some fresh air. I met Lucy coming out of the elevator, and we went straight outside.

"Did you audition?"

Lucy crossed her eyes. "Oh man, I did, I did, but I was so lucky. It was by the skin of my teeth. The one teacher, Frances, from masterclass, saw me at the back of the line of like a hundred people, and she said 'Aren't you supposed to be getting your results soon?', and I nodded, and she pulled me to the front. It went well, I hope."

"Awesome!" I said, giving her a high five.

Then I told her about everything that had been happening in my competition.

"How can these girls laugh at people falling over?" I asked.

"Yeah, some of these girls are real bitches. You want to know the real reason?"

I nodded.

"It's because some of those fallers are normally top twenty dancers." I shook my head in disgust. "Ok, I gotta run. My results are due any minute."

I wished her good luck as she went back inside. I stayed outside in the crisp Chicago air for another little while praying to the universe for a good end to a great day.

Chapter 46

I waited in the hall for over an hour until all of a sudden, people started cramming in. Lucy and Mrs. Gallagher came and joined me. Lucy was so red in the face. She had finished thirteenth. It was bittersweet for her—she had missed out on qualifying for Worlds by one place. We hardly had any time to talk as the room fell silent and the lights dimmed, and a monitor dropped down with a grid of dancer numbers and adjudicators at the top. All the recalled dancers were gathered in clumps with their teachers and moms. The red-dressed announcer lady from before got on stage with her microphone and started calling names and numbers.

"First judge, Paula Sweeney, results. Number 103, fifty points. Number 121, sixty-five."

The scores began to appear on the big grid; everyone's eyes locked in concentration. It felt like just numbers and numbers and more mind-numbingly confusing visuals and became impossible to keep up with who was doing well and who was who. There were bursts of cheers all around, and some faces were getting real excited.

The first judge gave me thirty-seven points, and the second judge gave me eight. After that, I started not really caring. Eight points felt like I may as well not have even tried. I looked over at Lucy, who watched in earnest. She nodded enthusiastically at me to keep watching, but I didn't feel like it. Jessica Harvey fist-pumped the air as she got two one-hundreds in a row.

I exhaled long and slow and began to daydream about what would happen next, how in the following days, Lucas and I would pack our bags, and Buck would bring us to the Greyhound station, and we'd be in Grandpa's house, making up beds in different bedrooms and starting out all fresh. And then I'd see Vinnie and his new girlfriend, and that made me think about Don and how I'd miss him.

After ages and ages of number-calling, I heard Mrs. G. and Lucy murmuring to each other. But I closed my eyes and got back to my daydream state and congratulated myself and thanked the universe for giving me the opportunity to dance at a major championship and for the wonderful few months Lucas and I had in Lakewood.

Then all of a sudden, Lucy poked me hard in the ribs, and I jumped back to reality. She was holding her phone with a calculator app open. Her face was beetroot.

"You have to go stand side stage with all the girls." I shrugged whatever, but Lucy wouldn't accept. "I'm serious, Alex, just go up there. I could be wrong, but just in case."

I glanced quickly at my number on the monitor and saw that the other judges had given me a fifteen, a twenty-eight and a twenty-two-point-five. I followed the other recalled girls side stage. The announcer continued.

"In first place, number 228, Jessica Harvey." Everyone clapped and cheered, and she went up on stage to collect her trophy and stand on the podium. This continued until the top ten were on stage. The announcer then said, "Congratulations to these ten world qualifiers."

Everyone clapped, including me. But that wasn't the end of it. One by one, they called up eleventh, then twelfth, and it kept going until top thirty were on stage getting medals placed 'round their necks. My hands were getting tired from clapping. Then next thing, the announcer said, "In thirty-second place, number 217, Alex Maslow."

I made this stunned face, but the rest of the girls side stage with me smiled hard and urged me up on stage.

"Nice job, Alex. So impressive for a beginner," said one girl with braces. I was all floaty as I ran up the steps and smiled like a goon as the lady shook my hand and said how well I had danced as I bowed down so she could place a medal 'round my neck. She then pointed to where I should stand, and I skipped over, squeezing the metal coin until it was warm with energy. But the biggest surprise was yet to come. The announcer spoke again.

"A round of applause for these thirty-two girls, who have qualified for North American Nationals."

There was a serious overreaction from the girls by my side, who started hollering and hugging and jumping around. I smiled and clapped for myself. I understood that it was an incredible achievement for me but also knew it didn't really matter, seeing as it would be close to impossible for me to go to Nans once I was back in Kentucky.

I floated back down the steps. Mrs. Gallagher embraced me, and Lucy lifted me and swung me around, and I felt wonderful.

I called home and told Kate. She hollered and hollered over the phone. "Don't forget to audition, Alex. It's your lucky day." I guessed she had a point.

I turned to Lucy. "Hey, you think there's time for me to audition?"

"It's like six PM now. I guess Mom might be happy to wait 'til like eight before driving home."

Excitedly, we both got in the elevator to the third floor, but my newfound enthusiasm was zapped when we saw a crowded hallway in every single direction. I looked at Lucy, and she pouted at me. There was no chance of squeezing in an audition.

"Never mind," I sang as we went back downstairs. Lucy saw a friend and went to say hi, and I saw a non-friend—Jessica Harvey—who was getting pictures taken with lots of people in the foyer. When she saw me, she walked by with her smug-ball face.

"Who you have to sleep with to get top thirty, southern belle?" She winked and saw Kal McGettigan coming toward her. He congratulated her and kissed her on the cheek. He abruptly stepped aside and made his way over to me.

He shook my hand courteously. "That is such an achievement, Alex. You must be so proud."

"Um, I am. I really am. I'm more shocked than anything, honestly."

"I can see that." He smiled glowingly. "I'm not entirely sure about this retro look." He nodded toward my dress.

"Um, yeah, it was all I could afford."

"You know my announcement is coming later tonight. Are you staying around?"

"No, my ride is leaving tonight…"

"That's too bad. Well, in that case, I'll let you in on a little secret."

But just then, his cell phone rang, and he had to take the call. He kept talking on his phone, walking over to Diane, tapping her on the shoulder and pointing at me before getting in the elevator. He waved at me as the doors closed. Diane, wearing skin-tight white trousers and a black turtleneck and heels, sauntered across.

"Alex, your reel was gorgeous. You're getting so strong. And you have a lovely way about you when you're on stage. Well done you," she said in her lilting Irish accent.

Then she pulled out her notebook.

"Do you mind if I take your details, maybe your email, home address and mobile number?"

"Um, sure," I said, and paused a second. "Not tryna be smart, but may I ask why?"

"Did Kal not tell you?"

I shook my head. "Tell me what?"

"Oh right. Well, keep this to yourself for the next few hours. He'll be making his announcement later. The big news is that he's bringing *Reel Rebels* to the US! He loves your story…He loves how you only started dancing six months ago and how much passion you have, how you taught yourself and how far you've come already."

"What? You can't be serious." I whimpered, shaking my head. "I didn't even audition."

"You don't have to audition. He thinks people will love your story."

I didn't know what to say. Finally, I mumbled, "But where? When?"

"In Cleveland. Sometime in January; we aren't exactly sure yet. So are you interested?"

"Holy. Shit!" I said those words real slow. Diane burst out laughing. Out of the corner of my eye, I spotted Jessica Harvey giving me sideways bitch eyes.

"Um, it sounds awesome. Can I think about it?"

"Sure."

I gave her my deets, and we parted ways. As I bounced towards Mrs. Gallagher and Lucy, I intentionally walked by Jessica Harvey.

"See you later, Chicago," I said, flashing my pearly whites at her. She did not like that.

Lucy grabbed hold of my two hands and stared deep into my eyes.

"OMG, Alex. What did Kal say? What did Diane say?"

My eyes lit up. "Holy crap, Lucy."

"Did Kal McGettigan ask you to be in a show?" she asked, on the verge of exploding.

"No, no, no."

"What then?"

"He said he wanted me for *Real Rebels USA*."

Lucy clapped her mouth. "He's bringing *Reel Rebels* to America?"

I nodded excitedly. Then we hugged.

Chapter 47

The ride back to Cleveland was a heavenly haze. Lucy and Joan could not stop talking about how well the trip had gone. Lucy didn't care too much that she hadn't qualified for Worlds because she wasn't going to go that following April anyway, and we talked and talked about *Reel Rebels USA* and how exciting that would be in the coming months. I had to protest hard when Joan tried to call some of the other dance moms to tell them the news.

"Please don't, Joan. He'll kill me. He'll know I was the one who let the secret slip."

"Gosh, Alex. We have so much work to do in dance class now. Guess you better ask Declan to come up with some cool steps to perform for the TV series. Guess we're pretty lucky he just arrived. Gosh, I hope I get a callback too." said Lucy, her thoughts verbally in overdrive. And I remembered I hadn't told Lucy my other news. If I had a choice I'd always chose sweet over bitter.

The moon shone big and bright in a cloudless, starry sky, and magic tingled through my body as I thought the happy thoughts. I fought hard not to think about the real stuff. It was truly amazing, what had happened over the past few months—the security, the friendships and the love that had grown in my mind and body. But the real truth was that Lucas and I would return to live with Grandpa and those dance dreams would have to be put aside. I drifted off into a tingly sleep, to a world and time where the possibility existed of all my hopes and dreams coming true.

The End

About the author

Seán de Gallaí first took an interest in writing in 2007 after taking a scriptwriting course. In 2011 he attended the Faber Academy in Dublin. His first book — *The Dancer. Steps from The Dark* — was published in 2015. In 2016 he released *Step Sisters*. *Making Moves* is his third book and the sequel to *The Dancer. Steps from the Dark*. Seán is a primary school teacher and works in Dublin. Purchase Seán's books at:

https://www.amazon.com/s/ref=nb_sb_noss_2?url=search-alias%3Daps&field-keywords=sean+de+gallai

seandegallai@gmail.com